THE CURSE
OF THE DEMON

OTHER YEARLING BOOKS YOU WILL ENJOY:

YEARLING BOOKS/YOUNG YEARLINGS/YEARLING CLASSICS
are designed especially to entertain and enlighten
young people. Patricia Reilly Giff, consultant to this
series, received the bachelor's degree from Mary-
mount College. She holds the master's degree in
history from St. John's University, and a professional
diploma in reading from Hofstra University. She was
a teacher and reading consultant for many years,
and is the author of numerous books for young
readers.

THE CURSE
OF THE DEMON

Mary Anderson

A YEARLING BOOK

Published by
Dell Publishing
a division of
Bantam Doubleday Dell Publishing Group, Inc.
666 Fifth Avenue
New York, New York 10103

The trademark Yearling® is registered in the U.S. Patent and Trademark Office.

ISBN: 0-440-40203-4

Printed in the United States of America

August 1989

10 9 8 7 6 5 4 3 2

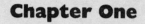

Chapter One

"ARE YOU STARING AT YOUR STUPID FACE AGAIN?"
Barney Prescott asked his cousin Cassie.

"I'm trying on this necklace. Isn't it beautiful?"
Cassie ran the jade beads through her fingers.

"Get your clammy hands off that. It's not yours,"
said Barney.

"This jade brings out the green in my eyes,
doesn't it?"

Days had passed since Barney'd had a good
fight with Cassie, and he was itching for one. "It
brings out the green in your skin, too. Put it back
or I'll tell Aunt Al you're messing in her room."

"You're not my boss. I can come in here whenever I like," said Cassie.

1

"But you can't snoop," Barney argued. "Aunt Alex invited us here for a year of fun and adventure, not *snooping*. When we signed that paper promising we'd stick together, it didn't say anything about snooping. So get out of here!"

"Buzz off," said Cassie. "I have to take orders from Crenshaw because he's our tutor, but you're *nothing*, wimpo—remember that, *nothing*." Cassie admired herself in the mirror. "Aunt Alex has gorgeous jewelry. Such *bon goût*."

"Bone goo?"

"That's French, stupid. It means 'good taste.' "

"Excuse me!"

"You're getting on my nerves, Prescott. What's it your business what I'm doing in here, anyway? Are you so perfect or what?"

Barney smiled smugly. "Yes, I am. I'm as perfect as a boy can be; my mom always says so."

Cassie groaned. "If you live a thousand years, you'll be far from perfect, Pressie."

"And you'll be far from bearable, Cass."

Cassie grabbed a pillow from Aunt Alex's bed and threw it, but it missed Barney.

Oliver Crenshaw passed by the door. The pillow hurtled by and hit him in the face. "What's the meaning of this?" he shouted. "Explain your juvenile behavior."

"*I* didn't do anything," said Barney innocently.

"I tried getting Cassie out of Aunt Al's room. I think she's taking things."

"He's a liar!" Cassie shouted. "Don't believe him!"

Crenshaw tossed the pillow onto the bed. "Cassie, I've been your tutor for almost a year. I know you can be mean, spiteful, impatient, lazy, and rude. But you'd never steal anything."

"Thanks a heap, that's hardly a compliment!"

Crenshaw grabbed Barney's shoulder. "I also know you can be too perfect for your own good. What're you up to?"

"Me? Nothing. I just don't think Cassie should wear Aunt Alex's stuff."

Crenshaw agreed. "That's a valuable necklace, young lady. Do you have your aunt's permission to wear it?"

"I'm just looking at it," she argued. "Why turn this into a cause célèbre?"

"Save that sappy French junk for boarding school," snapped Barney. "Let's forget it, okay? I guess Cassie wasn't stealing anything."

"You're both coming downstairs with me," said Crenshaw. "One of you is always up to something, but I can never figure out which. Let Alex decide." As they hurried down the stairs, Nora, the housekeeper, stood in the entrance hall. "Have you seen Mrs. Ludlington?" asked Crenshaw.

3

Nora looked grim. She pointed toward the library. "She's in there, sir. Madame has been in there all day. She didn't eat her lunch, and she didn't drink her tea. I'm getting worried."

"Is she sick?" asked Barney.

"She's *addicted*," said Nora somberly. "Why didn't I recognize the symptoms? I shouldn't have let that package in the house. I should've known what would happen if she started up again."

"Started up with what?" asked Cassie.

"*Whodunits*," said Nora grimly.

Crenshaw gasped. "Oh, no! I thought Alex was cured of that!"

Nora shook her head sadly. "Madame has the fever again, sir. She subscribed to the Mystery Madness Club last week and got a stack of books in the mail. She's been reading like crazy ever since. There's no stopping her now."

"This *is* serious," Crenshaw agreed.

"What's wrong with Aunt Alex reading mysteries?" asked Cassie.

"It can be *dangerous*," he explained. "Once Alex starts, she can't put them down. It nearly drove her late husband, Hugo, crazy! Poor Alex *never* solves the crimes, and that makes her furious." Crenshaw approached the library door. "Let's see how bad it is this time." As he pushed it open, a book came hurtling at him from across the room.

4

"No wonder they call this the Mystery Madness Club!" Aunt Alex shouted. "It makes me so mad when I don't guess whodunit!"

Crenshaw quickly ducked, but the book hit him in the face anyway.

Aunt Alex hurried toward him. "Sorry, Ollie, did I hurt you?"

"Forget it, Alex. I'm an easy target today."

"Cassie threw a pillow at him," said Barney.

"He's lying," said Cassie.

Aunt Alex picked up the book and hurled it against the wall. "What a gyp! How could Mrs. Murphy be the murderer? She couldn't have shot Dr. Harrow, because her arm was broken. I want my money back!"

Barney laughed. "Quit kidding. You're the richest woman in the country, Aunt Alex."

"I didn't get what I paid for," said Aunt Alex. "My late husband, Hugo, insisted everyone get what he paid for. He became a *millionaire* by treating people fairly, but I feel gypped!" Aunt Alex smiled at Cassie and Barney. "Take our agreement. Now that was a *fair* exchange. I get your charming company for a year. In return, you get to take trips to exciting places."

"What about *my* part in the bargain?" asked Crenshaw.

"You get to tutor the children, Ollie."

5

"That's what I mean," he replied. "I think *I've* been gypped, too."

Aunt Alex grinned. "You know you *love* teaching the children, Ollie. Stop pretending you dislike it."

"Who's pretending? Don't make it sound as if I *enjoy* this job. I'm doing it only for friendship, Alex. I've always taken care of your business interests."

"*I'm* not a business interest," said Barney. "I'm a 'charming young man' like my mom always says."

Aunt Alex threw her book on the table angrily. "I still think I've been gypped. I was promised a spine-tingling mystery, but I got a *dud*."

"That's sour grapes," said Crenshaw. "Admit it, Alex, you *never* guess whodunit."

"You're entitled to your opinion, Ollie, even if it's wrong. I've solved lots of mysteries in my day."

"Name one," he asked. "No, never mind, let's not argue. I've come to tell you Cassie was poking around in your bedroom. Did you give her permission?"

"Cassie can poke around if she likes," said Aunt Alex.

"But she was *snooping*," said Barney.

"Guests always snoop, especially in fancy houses.

When Hugo and I first moved in here, *I* snooped, too. I couldn't believe a house could have so many rooms! Did you find any dust balls under the carpets, Cassie?"

"Cassie didn't snoop under the carpets," said Barney. "She snooped in your *drawers.*"

"Cassie is probably bored," said Aunt Alex. "And so am I! We've been poking around the house too long. We need to take another trip. There's still time for one more journey before you children leave. How about it, Ollie? Should we give the children a final big send-off?"

"I've love to send them off," said Crenshaw. "I want to return to being your business manager. But while Cassie and Barney are here, they must obey rules. Did you allow Cassie to go through your jewelry box?"

Aunt Alex stared at Cassie. "Goodness, you're wearing my *jade necklace.*"

"I told her she shouldn't," said Barney smugly. "It's real valuable, right?"

"It's the most precious thing I own," said Aunt Alex.

Barney poked Cassie. "I *told* you."

"I didn't hurt it," said Cassie. "The necklace looked so beautiful, I had to try it. The jade complements my green eyes and blond hair."

Aunt Alex sighed dreamily. "That's what Hugo

7

said when he bought it for *me*. I remember as if it were yesterday. We were sight-seeing on our honeymoon in Mexico. We wandered down a quaint street and discovered a charming curio shop. I fell in love with the necklace in the window, and Hugo insisted I have it. It cost a fortune! The shopkeeper kept insisting it belonged to an *ancient princess*. And Hugo kept insisting it made *me* look like a princess." She wiped a tear from her eye. "Dear Hugo."

Barney nudged Cassie again. "Look, you've made Aunt Alex sad, thinking about poor old Hugo."

"No, I'm *never* sad thinking of Hugo," she insisted. "Our life together was wonderful!"

Barney was practically drooling. "Will you *punish* Cassie for taking the necklace?"

"No," said Aunt Alex, "I think I'll *give* Cassie the necklace."

Barney was stunned. *"What?"*

Cassie was overjoyed. "Are you *serious*, Aunt Alex?"

"Yes, but the necklace has too much sentimental value to part with it immediately. I think I'll give it to you on your twenty-first birthday."

"But that's *ten years* from now!" said Cassie.

"I'll let you wear it sometimes, but you can't have it until you've grown up," explained Aunt Alex.

8

Barney laughed. "That means you'll *never* get that necklace, Cass. You'll always be too *juvenile* to qualify."

"And you'll always be a *wimp*," Cassie shouted. "When you're eighty, you'll be an old wrinkled wimp!"

Aunt Alex smiled. "I'll miss these wonderful fights when you children leave. They keep me feeling young. Won't you miss them, too, Ollie?"

"Not for a moment," said Crenshaw.

Aunt Alex nudged him. "Admit it, Ollie, the children keep *you* young, too."

"They keep me exhausted," he argued. "My advice is that our next trip be strictly *educational*."

"No, strictly *fun*," said Barney.

"Gaining knowledge can be fun," said Crenshaw. "Why do you think I was listed in the *Guinness Book* as the world's smartest man? Because acquiring knowledge is a *pleasure*."

Cassie was more interested in acquiring the jade necklace. "Must I wait *ten years*, Aunt Alex?"

"I'm afraid so. It'll be something to look forward to, dear."

Cassie couldn't look forward to returning to boarding school. There she felt unnoticed and unloved. Feeling the beads against her skin, she felt special. She *loved* the necklace. Something so won-

9

derful was *worth* waiting for. "Can I wear it on our last trip together, Aunt Alex?"

"Maybe we shouldn't *plan* our last journey," said Aunt Alex. "Something always pops up, doesn't it, Ollie?"

"Unfortunately, that's true," he said.

"Then that's settled," said Aunt Alex. "Our last journey will be like all our others—unexpected."

"Our *last journey*?" asked Barney. "I don't like the sound of that."

"Neither do I," said Crenshaw. "It's too solemn and deadly."

Aunt Alex hurried toward the bookshelf. "That reminds me, I've enough time to read another whodunit before dinner!"

Chapter Two

"I *HATE* LESSONS," SAID CASSIE. SHE AND BARNEY SAT in Aunt Alex's library with their books scattered across the table. "No matter where we are, we have lessons. Whenever we take a trip, we still have lessons. And every country we visit, we have lessons. It's not fair!"

Barney agreed. "This is our year for fun and adventure!"

"And *study*," Crenshaw added. "Your lessons are almost over for today. Only twenty more minutes of math."

"I can't stand twenty seconds more," said Cassie. "This isn't a *real* classroom anyway. And you're not a real teacher."

"Crenshaw is *smarter* than a real teacher," said Barney coyly. "He's smarter than *anyone*."

"Too smart to be sweet-talked," said Crenshaw. "Finish your math, both of you."

Cassie sighed dramatically. "First, I need some fresh air." She hurried to the window and looked out. "There's someone *weird* standing outside."

"I know all your diversions, Cassie, so none of your tricks," said Crenshaw.

"It's not a trick," said Cassie. She stared down toward the entrance. An odd-looking old man with strange, piercing eyes stared back. Cassie shuddered, then turned away. "Honest, there's a really creepy man standing outside. He looks like a *mummy!*"

"Describe him," said Barney.

"He has a flat head covered with long black hair, and he's got jewelry stuck through his nose."

"Yeah, sure."

"See for yourself," said Cassie.

Barney hurried toward the window. "Hey, there *is* someone out there." He stared at the strange old man. Their unexpected visitor had dark copper-colored skin, and he wore a brilliant topaz set in the side of his long, bent nose. "Look, he's got pointed ears, too. And he's wearing earrings in them!" The old man's hair was deep black and braided into a wreath around his head. As the man stared up at the window, Barney noticed his eyes were severely crossed. "You're right, Cass, that's a weird-looking guy. You suppose he's from another country?"

"I think he's from another *planet*," she said.

Crenshaw was growing curious. He hurried to the window, too. "That fellow looks familiar. Where have I seen his face before?"

"It must've been in a *nightmare*," said Cassie.

"Why is he snooping around down there?" asked Crenshaw.

The old man finally rang the bell, and Crenshaw ran down the stairs to open the door. "Can I help you?"

As the old man bowed, his aging bones seemed ready to crack. His thin, high-pitched voice sounded as if it were traveling through a tunnel. "I am seeking Mrs. Ludlington."

"I'm her business manager. Can I help you?"

"My name is Mr. K. Kulcan," he explained. "I have been sent here as an emissary of the Mexican peoples."

"I knew you must have come from far away," said Barney.

Mr. Kulcan nodded. "Yes, if one considers time a place, I have come from *very* far away."

Crenshaw ushered the old man inside. "How may we help you? Did you say you're a government man?"

"I represent the ancient Mesoamerican peoples. I've come on a matter of urgency and I must see Mrs. Ludlington immediately. Many lives hang in the balance."

"That sounds serious," said Crenshaw. "What's the problem?"

Mr. Kulcan looked solemn. "It regards a jade necklace in her possession."

Cassie suddenly felt threatened by the old man. "What about the necklace?"

"Mrs. Ludlington must give it to me. It's a matter of life and death!"

Aunt Alex put down her cup. "Now that we've had tea, please tell me why you've come, Mr. Kulcan."

"He wants my necklace," said Cassie. "Tell him he can't have it, Aunt Alex."

"I thought the necklace was *yours*, Mrs. Ludlington."

"*How* did you know that?" asked Aunt Alex.

"Yes, who told you?" asked Cassie.

"I've seen the records of the antiques dealer in Mexico," Mr. Kulcan explained.

"So what?" said Cassie. "That necklace is mine now—or almost mine, isn't it, Aunt Alex?"

"That's right. I've promised Cassie she'll inherit the necklace on her twenty-first birthday."

"No one can inherit someone else's property," said Mr. Kulcan.

"But it's *my* property," said Aunt Alex. "I can give it to Cassie if I like."

"It's *not* yours," Mr. Kulcan argued.

"What's that mean?" asked Cassie.

"It means my people believe the dead don't rest until they're avenged. I've come here to prepare a path, or else you'll all suffer the wrath of the vengeful one!"

"That sounds *mysterious*," said Aunt Alex.

Mr. Kulcan placed his cup on the table. "May I tell you all a story?"

"Is it a whodunit?" asked Barney. "Aunt Alex *loves* mysteries. Nora says she's addicted to them."

Mr. Kulcan's dark eyes gleamed. "This is an unsolved mystery from beyond the great tombs of the past. And *you* have the power to solve it."

"How fascinating," said Aunt Alex.

"Unfortunately, it is also a story of treachery and deceit," he added. "It happened fifty-two years ago while archaeologists were digging near Tikal in the Guatemalan jungle. Tikal, one of the great Mayan city-states, was lost to the world for centuries."

"How come?" asked Barney.

"It was hidden away by centuries of jungle vegetation. But after scholars labored for years, doz-

15

ens of temple pyramids were uncovered and many burial crypts were unearthed."

Crenshaw nodded. "Yes, ancient tombs were opened, weren't they?"

"Yes, many glyphs and stelae verified that Tikal had been a great metropolis," said Mr. Kulcan proudly. "But many glyphs have yet to be deciphered."

"What are glyphs and stelae?" asked Barney.

"They're like Egyptian hieroglyphics," Crenshaw explained.

"Did ancient Mexicans have mummies, tombs, and all that scary stuff, too?"

"Yes," said Mr. Kulcan. "Many mysteries still shroud the Olmec and Toltec cultures, just as mysteries of ancient Egyptian life have yet to be unlocked."

"It's true I love mysteries," said Aunt Alex, "but what's this have to do with my necklace?"

"The gods were pleased at the unearthing of the Temple of the Great Jaguar," said Mr. Kulcan. "But later the gods grew angry because burial sites were looted by the greedy. Once again priceless information was lost to civilization."

"What was stolen?" asked Aunt Alex.

"Recently ancient glyphs have been deciphered, and scholars have compiled a list of the objects," Mr. Kulcan explained. "The entire tomb of a royal princess was looted. Pearl, turquoise, emerald, and gold jewelry was stolen. The most precious piece was a jade necklace, said to be made from stones belonging to Quetzalcoatl."

"Ketzywho?" asked Barney.

"Quetzalcoatl is a great god," said Mr. Kulcan.

"Do gods wear *jewelry*?" asked Barney.

"Gods do whatever they please," said Mr. Kulcan. "My people revered jade. The tiniest pieces were saved and put into the mouths of the dead to replace their stilled hearts. So you see, the necklace is priceless and must be returned."

"You can't mean *my* jade necklace," said Cassie defensively.

"Do you think it was *stolen* from the excavation?" asked Aunt Alex. "That's impossible. Hugo *bought* it for me."

"That necklace was stolen from the tomb," said Mr. Kulcan.

"I don't believe that," said Cassie.

"It must be returned!" Mr. Kulcan insisted.

"Hold it," said Crenshaw. "Legally speaking, possession is nine-tenths of the law."

"I don't speak legally," Mr. Kulcan replied sharply. "If these artifacts aren't returned, the pieces of the past will never fit together properly. The gods won't rest! Everything must be returned before the moon's next cycle. I have spoken!"

Barney winced. "What's that, a *curse* or something?"

"It sounds more like a *threat*," said Aunt Alex.

Mr. Kulcan apologized. "I forget you don't understand my culture. The ancient peoples believed time goes in cycles. Each fifty-two years a cycle is repeated. If all things aren't put right by the end of each cycle, there are disastrous consequences. Everything stolen from the tomb must be returned before the fifteenth of this month. That's exactly fifty-two years since the excavation was looted."

"*Alex* didn't loot anything," Crenshaw protested.

"You can't defy the gods," Mr. Kulcan warned him.

"You can't defy logic either," said Crenshaw. "Why should Mrs. Ludlington believe you? Where's your proof? Where's your identification?"

"I have none," he admitted.

"Maybe you're a clever con man or a charlatan," Crenshaw suggested.

Mr. Kulcan was insulted. "Is that *your* opinion, madame?"

Aunt Alex shrugged. "I don't know *who* you are, but I can't give you the necklace. It belongs to Cassie now."

"*I* won't give it to you," said Cassie. "*Never*. No way!"

"Then I bid you good day," said Mr. Kulcan.

He walked toward the hall. "But I warn you," he added sharply, "my adversary isn't as tolerant. If things aren't put right, the gods will seek revenge. I fear the wrathful twin will come, so beware the demon with the mirrored foot!" He bowed solemnly, then slammed the door behind him.

"Did he say *demon*?" asked Barney. "What's that mean?"

"It sounds like another *curse*," said Crenshaw. "What a weird fellow."

"I think he's cuckoo," said Barney.

"And creepy," said Cassie. "I hope he never comes back."

Crenshaw scratched his chin thoughtfully. "Where have I seen his face before? His name sounds familiar, too. What did you think of him, Alex? Did you believe anything he said?"

"It's all very *mysterious*, isn't it?" said Aunt Alex. "Which reminds me, I still have time for one more whodunit before dinner!"

Chapter Three

"HOW MARVELOUS," SAID AUNT ALEX AS SHE READ her morning mail. "We've been invited to solve a *crime*."

"What crime?" asked Cassie.

"Quetzal Tours is offering a special cruise, and we're invited to guess whodunit."

"Who done *what*?" asked Barney.

"I don't know," said Aunt Alex, handing him the invitation:

SHARE OUR HISTORICAL MEXICAN
MYSTERY TOUR

Observe closely as a CRIME is committed!

20

Follow the clues
Examine the evidence
Question the witnesses
and
Solve the Mystery
WHO IS THE GUILTY PARTY?
WHAT IS THE DASTARDLY DEED?

(Professional actors will mingle with guests, so remember, *no one* is above suspicion!)

SOLVE THE CRIME AND WIN A TROPHY AS
MASTER DETECTIVE

Live it up!
Dress to kill!
Ethnic Mayan food
Entertainment
Lectures
Authentic Mayan sports
plus

A Costume Dance Party our final night at sea
(appropriate Mayan jewelry required)

"That's great," said Barney. "I've never been on a cruise before. I'll get to see the galley and poop deck and all that nautical stuff. And I can play sports on board, too; that's terrific."

Cassie read the invitation. "Cruises can be so *romantic*. There's always moonlight on the water and music playing in the lounge. I'd love to go to the Costume Dance Party. Can I wear my jade necklace? Maybe I'll meet a charming young man on board."

Barney laughed. "He'll run a mile when he sees you."

Cassie passed the invitation to Crenshaw. "This sounds very educational," he said. "There'll be several lectures, so I won't have to tutor the children. And I'd love to learn more about Mexican culture."

"Don't forget the best part," said Aunt Alex. "We'll get to solve a *crime* during this three-day cruise around the Yucatán Peninsula. I can snoop around and discover clues. It's like a *living* mystery novel. That's something I've always dreamed about."

"Yes, I think this ocean voyage makes a wonderful last journey," said Crenshaw.

"Who sent us the invitation?" asked Cassie.

"Whoever it was knows exactly what we like," said Barney.

"You're right," agreed Crenshaw. "It's the ideal trip for *all* of us. Who sent the invitation, Alex?"

"I don't know," said Aunt Alex. "Our host is anonymous."

"How strange," said Crenshaw.

"I think it's exciting," said Aunt Alex. "Not knowing who sent the invitation adds to the mystery. Everything is settled. The winds are taking us to the Yucatán Peninsula!"

"Not more *ruins*," Barney grumbled. "Crenshaw, why do you show us ruins wherever we go?"

"Our future is locked in our past, young man, remember that."

As Crenshaw drove through the city of Mérida, Cassie sat in the back seat enjoying the ride. She wasn't interested in sight-seeing. She looked forward to the dance party on board ship, where she could show off her necklace and meet a handsome young man. "When does our mystery cruise begin?" she asked eagerly.

"Not until this evening," Aunt Alex explained. "We have the whole day to explore the Yucatán. Aren't we lucky?"

As Cassie stared out the window, she saw the clean white Spanish colonial buildings of Mérida. Once they'd driven through the city, the scenery changed. Approaching the ruins of Chichén Itzá, they passed several Mayan villages starkly simple and primitive.

Barney yawned. "It's too *early* to look at ruins. I've got jet lag, and I haven't had breakfast."

Cassie agreed. "Why must we start sight-seeing so *early*?"

"By afternoon busloads of tourists will be here," Crenshaw explained.

"If it's crowded, let's skip it," said Barney.

"You can't come to the Yucatán and not visit the ruins," Crenshaw argued.

"We could *try*," said Cassie.

"Alex, you love mysteries," said Crenshaw. "Tell the children the Mayan ruins hold the biggest mystery in history."

"Do they, Ollie? I didn't know that."

"It's true," he told them. "No one knows what happened to the ancient Mayan civilization. Why did they build these huge cities, then abandon them? What happened? What do their ancient hieroglyphics mean? Not even modern computers have been able to decipher most of them. And why did they abandon their entire advanced culture? Was it a plague? A drought? An invasion? No one knows."

"Aunt Al needs mysteries with *clues*," said Barney.

Crenshaw glanced ahead as the ruins of Chichén Itzá came into view. "There are lots of clues etched into those monuments, but we don't know how to decipher them."

"Maybe you're right, Ollie," said Aunt Alex. "Maybe Chichén Itzá is one of the world's *true* mysteries."

Chapter Four

IT WAS 8:00 A.M. WHEN THEY ARRIVED AT THE GATES OF Chichén Itzá.

As they stood in front of the ancient buildings, Barney felt insignificant. He stared at the temples, pyramids, and massive structures. "Why is everything so *big*?"

"The Mayans built on a grand scale, just like the Egyptians." Crenshaw pointed to a huge site in the central plaza of the ruined city. "That's El Castillo, a temple honoring the god Quetzalcoatl, known as the plumed serpent."

"That's the one Mr. Kulcan mentioned," said Barney. He hurried toward the base of the pyramid, then ran up the steps. When he reached the

25

top, he ran down again. "I'll bet you could play a great game of catch from up there."

Cassie, Crenshaw, and Aunt Alex climbed different sides of the pyramid. At the summit they had a panoramic view of a temple with nine terraces.

"What's that big one over there?" asked Barney.

"That's the ball court," said Crenshaw. "It's twice the size of a football field."

"Did ancient Mayans play football? Did they wear shoulder pads and helmets?"

"Their game was more like soccer," Crenshaw explained. "They played it with a rubber ball."

Barney couldn't wait to see the ball court up closer. He was fascinated by the stone banquettes on the sides of the court. He stared at the engravings. "What a yucky picture!" One ballplayer was depicted on his knees. "Look, his head's been cut off, and that other player is holding it in the air. What's it mean?"

"He's the loser in the ball game," said Crenshaw. "Mayans took their sports *seriously*."

"You must be joking," said Aunt Alex.

"No, the losing team was put to death," said Crenshaw. "Human sacrifice was part of the Mayan belief."

The hot sun beamed down as Aunt Alex and the children followed Crenshaw across the Great

Plaza, then over a narrow causeway, where they approached a well filled with green water.

"This is the Well of Sacrifice," he explained. "Here, in times of drought, people were offered up to the rain god Chac."

"You mean they were *killed*?" asked Cassie.

"They were flung from the top of the pyramid. But the Mayans believed they didn't actually die."

"Mayans were awfully *stupid*," said Cassie.

"No, they had an advanced knowledge of mathematics and astronomy," said Crenshaw.

"That makes them smarter than you, Cass," said Barney.

"Then why did they *murder* people?" asked Cassie.

"People weren't sacrificed out of cruelty," said Crenshaw. "The Mayans hoped human sacrifice would bring back the gift of water. The gods *always* had to be satisfied."

Cassie felt nauseated. "It's a good thing we didn't eat breakfast yet. I would've lost mine."

"Mayans seemed preoccupied with *death*," said Aunt Alex, noticing a row of skulls along a carved stone wall.

"Some of those skulls are so small," said Cassie. "Did Mayans sacrifice *children*, too?"

"Yes, maidens and infants were also cast into the whirlpool," said Crenshaw.

27

"I don't like this place," said Cassie.

"You're *scared*," said Barney. "You have a wimpy stomach, Cass. What's wrong, don't you like blood sacrifices?"

"I don't like *mass murder*," said Cassie.

"I'll bet there was blood everywhere." Barney teased her. "Blood oozing all over. And I'll bet *you'd* be the first to get killed, Cass. You'd be in that water hole quick as a flash, dead in the water!"

"You're here to *learn* something, Barney," said Aunt Alex.

"I have learned something," he said. "Being a Mayan was hazardous to your health. I'll bet that's how they all got wiped out. They bumped each other off! Hey, maybe I've solved the mystery of the ancient Mayans!"

"Good, now we can leave," said Cassie.

"Not until we've seen the Temple of the Warriors," said Crenshaw. He led them toward a structure set upon a stepped platform, surrounded by columns. At its base were several huge reclining figures, each holding a platelike shape on its stomach. "These are called Chac-Mools," he explained.

"Snack bowls?" asked Barney.

"No, *Chac-Mools*. The bowls they hold weren't for snacks, Barney. Human hearts were placed inside—the still-beating hearts of sacrificed victims!"

Cassie hurried away to look at some wall paint-

28

ings. When she saw the faces staring down at her, she gasped and ran to get Aunt Alex. "Look, all these drawings resemble that scary old man!"

Aunt Alex inspected the murals. Every figure had crossed eyes and a flattened head. "Yes, they all look like Mr. Kulcan."

"No wonder he looked familiar," said Crenshaw.

"Do all Mayans look like that?" asked Cassie.

"Only *ancient* Mayans," he explained.

"Why do Mayans have crossed eyes and flat foreheads?" asked Aunt Alex.

"That was fashionable a thousand years ago."

"You mean they weren't born that way?" asked Barney.

"No, a Mayan mother would hang a ball in front of her baby's face until its eyes were crossed," Crenshaw explained.

"That's gross," said Cassie.

"Then the baby's skull would be flattened by tying boards to it while the bones were still soft."

"Why?" asked Barney.

"The resulting shape was said to represent an ear of corn," said Crenshaw. "Mayans worshiped corn."

"I still don't understand," said Cassie. "Why does Mr. Kulcan look that way? He's not a thousand years old."

"He looked *two thousand!*" said Barney.

29

Crenshaw shrugged. "Who knows? Nothing about Mr. Kulcan makes sense to me."

"Can we leave now?" asked Cassie.

"Scared?" asked Barney. "Afraid a Mayan mummy will get you?"

"I think we've seen enough ruins," said Aunt Alex. "Let's return to Mérida and go to the beach."

Chapter Five

THE CRUISE SHIP *QUETZAL* LAY AT ANCHOR IN THE GULF. Night had fallen, the harbor was dark, and the ship's twinkling lights sparkled across the dense blue water.

Aunt Alex glanced around the long promenade deck, which was silent. "Isn't this *mysterious*? Keep your eyes open and consider *everything* a clue. Nothing on board is what it seems to be, so remember, be suspicious of *everyone*."

Cassie stopped midway up the gangplank. "I don't like this ship," she whispered. "It's too quiet and empty."

Barney pushed her up the gangplank. "Quit whining. Things look fine."

31

"How would *you* know, dumbo? You've never been on a cruise before. Ocean cruises have bright lights, music, gaiety. This looks like a *ghost ship*."

"Maybe everyone ran when they saw you coming," said Barney. "That handsome guy you're waiting to meet probably jumped overboard!"

Suddenly the captain appeared. "Welcome aboard, I'm Captain Merado. We'll soon be casting off from the Gulf of Mexico into the Yucatán Channel, then into the Caribbean Sea. My crew and I hope you enjoy your mystery cruise."

"Where are the other passengers?" asked Crenshaw.

"You're the first ones to board," he explained. "We'll have a dozen guests."

"Is that all?" asked Aunt Alex, staring up at the ship's three decks. "Such a large ship should have a hundred passengers."

"We usually do," said Captain Merado, "but this is an exclusive *private* charter."

A young man in a stiffly starched white uniform with brass buttons took their baggage. "I'm your steward, Miguel. Any questions?"

"Tell me all about the cruise," said Aunt Alex eagerly.

"The *Quetzal* uses a Mexican registry, a Mexican

32

flag, and a Central American crew. There's a main lounge, a promenade deck, smoking room, library, swimming pool, two bars, a movie theater, a restaurant on B deck, and—"

"No, I mean, when does the *mystery* begin? What's the crime? Did we miss any clues? Should we look for fingerprints?"

A fat, balding man rushed up the ramp, knocking into Aunt Alex. "Sorry, lady, gotta get to my cabin." He grabbed Miguel's arm. "Which way to my cabin, fella? I'm a landlubber and can't tell fore from aft."

Miguel checked his registry. "Are you Mr. Hackett?"

"Right, Charlie Hackett. I'm a hardware salesman from Columbus, Ohio."

"You're in stateroom twelve. I'll show you the way."

Mr. Hackett pushed Miguel aside. "No time for that, I'm in a big rush." Then he hurried away.

"Aha," said Aunt Alex, "that's our first *clue*. Mr. Hackett said he didn't know his way around a ship, but he headed straight for his cabin. Isn't that *suspicious?*"

"Was that really a clue?" asked Barney. "Captain, what kind of mystery do we have to solve?"

"Excuse me," said Captain Merado, "I must greet my other passengers."

An extremely snooty-looking woman was the next to come on board. "I'm Mrs. MacIntosh. Is my stateroom ready? Send someone to take my jewels to your safe."

"Sorry, madame, there's no purser on board," said Miguel.

"No purser? That's disgraceful!"

"We have a scaled-down crew because we have so few passengers," he explained.

"With such dreadful service, I'm surprised you have *any* passengers!" Mrs. MacIntosh hurried away to the stateroom.

"I'll bet that's another clue," said Aunt Alex.

Barney was getting confused. "What do *you* think, Crenshaw? Which ones are real passengers, and which ones are actors?"

"Who knows? Frankly, I think your aunt has gone *overboard*!"

"I heard that horrid pun, Ollie. Shall we make a friendly wager? I bet *I* solve this shipboard mystery first."

"I think something strange is going on," said Cassie.

"Of course there is," said Aunt Alex. "It's part of the plot. Look sharp, or you'll miss all the clues."

The next passenger to board was a young girl. Barney thought she was beautiful. Was *she* a clue, too? he wondered. She reminded Barney of a princess in a fairy tale with dark hair and a faraway look. As she walked along the deck, she smiled at Barney. It was the sweetest smile he'd ever received, and it turned him all squushy inside. He even *blushed*. No girl had *ever* made Barney blush! He turned away in embarrassment.

The girl was followed by a handsome teenage boy—the *handsomest* boy Cassie had ever seen!

"Who's that girl?" asked Barney dreamily.

"And who's the boy with her?" asked Cassie. "He looks too good to be true!"

"Those are the Esperanza children," said Miguel. "They're direct descendants of kings, so Nena and Juan have *royal* blood."

"I *knew* she must be a princess!" said Barney.

"Are they traveling alone?" asked Aunt Alex.

"Our host is their guardian," said Miguel.

"Who's our host?" asked Crenshaw.

"That's a secret," said Miguel.

"It's part of the mystery, isn't it?" asked Aunt Alex. "*Everything* is part of the mystery!"

"I've never met royalty before," said Cassie. "Can you introduce us?"

"I don't have time," said Miguel. "Our special entertainment will soon begin."

As Barney watched Nena and her brother depart, he couldn't get her face out of his mind. He

35

leaned against the ship's rail and stared into the inky blue water. The color reminded him of Nena's dark eyes, and each lapping ripple whispered her name. Barney felt like melting inside. Was this *love* or what? Was it possible? Could love strike so *quickly*?

"Is it a deal, Ollie?" asked Aunt Alex. "C'mon, put your money where your mouth is."

"I'll think about it," said Crenshaw.

"Be a sport, Ollie. I'm itching for a contest. Bet me I solve this mystery first."

"Why?"

"Because I'm determined to win the Master Detective Trophy," said Aunt Alex.

"Why?" asked Crenshaw.

"Because I've never won anything my entire life," she confessed. "Hugo was always winning prizes or awards. All my friends have won something, but I *never* have."

"I won a turkey in a raffle," said Barney.

"Once I won a goldfish," said Cassie, "but it died."

"I was listed in the *Guinness Book* as the world's smartest man," said Crenshaw proudly.

"You see?" said Aunt Alex. "You've all won something. I *need* that trophy, Ollie, and I plan to get it!"

"But, Alex, you don't even know what the mystery is yet."

"Whatever it is, I'll solve it," she insisted.

Cassie clutched her carrying case with the jade necklace inside. She was eager to wear it to the Costume Dance Party and hoped Juan would ask her to dance. "I don't care who solves the mystery. I'm looking forward to the *dance*."

Barney knew what was on her mind. "Don't hold your breath. That guy won't ask *you* to dance. I'll bet he dances only with royalty."

"I saw that sappy look you gave Nena, but she won't give you a second glance," said Cassie.

"You're wrong," Barney shouted. "Nena *smiled* at me."

"I'll bet she was delirious," said Cassie.

"And I'll bet I can win that trophy," said Aunt Alex. She nudged Crenshaw. "What do you say, Ollie? Will you take my bet?"

"All right, Alex, you win. I mean you're on!"

Cassie noticed a light from the upper deck. A cabin door slowly opened. Then a figure emerged. Cassie stared at the strange intruder tiptoeing toward the stairwell. He looked frightening, covered in feathers and paint. Snaky things protruded from his head, and he had the face of an animal. "Look up there," she shouted.

"Don't be frightened," said Captain Merado. "That's one of our dancers."

"Why is he dressed like that?" asked Cassie.

"He represents Quetzalcoatl," the captain explained. "The Mayans had many gods. Some were good; some were very evil. You'll learn about them *all* tonight."

Chapter Six

Dinner was very unusual: corn chowder, corn fritters, scalloped corn, corn relish, and corn pudding for dessert.

Barney mushed it around on his plate. "Aren't there any burgers on board?"

"Ancient Mayans and Aztecs lived on corn," explained Crenshaw. "They even had gods to honor corn, so this meal is very ethnic."

"It's also very boring," said Barney.

"Try the fritters," said Aunt Alex. "They're delicious."

Barney had no appetite. He was thinking about Nena and was anxious to see her again. The other passengers had come to dinner, but the Esperanza children were missing. Where was Nena? Was she seasick? Was she part of the mystery? What was *happening* to him? he wondered. Was this strange feeling love or hunger pains?

Aunt Alex glanced around the dining room, sizing up the other passengers. "Maybe someone will be *murdered* during dinner," she said hopefully. "Or maybe there will be a theft or a kidnapping."

Barney didn't like the sound of that. Had *Nena* been kidnapped? Was she in danger? Who'd dare harm anyone so beautiful? Anyway, it was all *pretend*. "This mystery junk is making me awfully nervous," he admitted.

"Me, too," said Cassie. "If something's going to happen, it'd better happen soon."

As the waiter cleared the tables, the dining room lights dimmed. Captain Merado made an announcement. "Our entertainment begins. Welcome our dancers."

The guests applauded as several dancers wearing grotesque makeup and exotic costumes appeared. They swirled between the tables, stamped their feet, flailed their arms, and chanted.

"Very ethnic," noted Crenshaw.

"Marvelous costumes," Aunt Alex added.

Each dancer represented an ancient Mayan god. They wore masks depicting eagles, jaguars, coyotes, and serpents. Suddenly two dancers emerged and engaged in hand-to-hand combat. One had a skull-like jaguar face with a mirror attached to one foot. The other had a serpent face covered with feathers. The jaguar wrestled the serpent to the ground.

"These are twin deities, Quetzalcoatl and Tezcatlipoca," explained the captain.

"They both look scary," Cassie whispered.

"And ugly," Barney added.

"Quetzalcoatl is called the plumed serpent," the captain continued. "He is a kindly god, but his brother is the demon with the mirrored foot. Tezcatlipoca can disguise himself as anything: an infant; an old man; a beautiful girl. He can trick people and drive them to their deaths. This is the wicked avenging god who will stop at nothing to get what he wants. Legend tells us these two are constantly battling for supremacy and always trying to trick each other."

Crenshaw chuckled. "They sound a lot like Cassie and Barney."

"That Tezzy god is the one Mr. Kulcan warned us about," said Barney. "He said that demon with the funny foot would seek *revenge* on us!"

"Do you think Mr. Kulcan *cursed* us?" asked Cassie.

"Don't be silly," said Aunt Alex. "Why would he do that?"

Barney couldn't miss a chance to scare Cassie. "Maybe Mr. Kulcan is a Mayan *mummy*, that's why. I'll bet he came out of his tomb to get back the jade necklace, so you'd better give it up, Cass."

Aunt Alex poked him. "Ssh, you're disturbing the performance."

"Legend tells us to beware these two adversaries," said Captain Merado. "When in combat, they can be terrifying disturbers of life."

"Yes, definitely like Cassie and Barney," said Crenshaw.

"Tezcatlipoca is a tricky demon," the captain concluded. "He can become *invisible*."

With a swirl of feathers the dancers finished. Then everyone applauded.

"That demon god sounds tough," said Barney. "Good thing he's only pretend."

"The Mayans believed he was *real*," said Crenshaw.

As the lights came back up, Cassie gasped in surprise. *Mr. Kulcan* was approaching their table.

Aunt Alex was surprised, too. "What are *you* doing on this cruise?"

Mr. Kulcan bowed. "*I'm* your host. You're all my guests on this cruise."

"So *you're* our mysterious benefactor," said Aunt Alex. "But we barely know you, Mr. Kulcan. *Why* would you treat us all to this cruise?"

"Since you love mysteries, perhaps you can *guess* why."

"There's something fishy here," said Crenshaw. "What are you up to?"

"Ollie, don't be impolite," said Aunt Alex. "We're Mr. Kulcan's guests. We've all been invited to guess whodunit."

"Have we? I'm not so sure. Maybe things aren't what they seem."

"Life is *never* what it seems," said Mr. Kulcan. "Unknown dangers always await us, so I beg you, give back the jade necklace before it's too late."

"So that's it," said Crenshaw. "We've been *lured* here, haven't we? What's the deal, blackmail?"

Cassie grew anxious to return to her cabin. She'd left the necklace locked in her jewelry box. Was it still there? she wondered.

As Barney stared at Mr. Kulcan, he realized he *did* look like a mummy!

"I've warned you," said Mr. Kulcan. "The gods *always* seek revenge. You can't escape their wrath. If you don't return the necklace, something of yours will be taken—something precious."

Crenshaw stood up. "I dislike threats. I think we all should leave this ship before it sails."

"It's too late for that," Mr. Kulcan informed him. "This ship has sailed. The captain already gave the order. We've cleared the harbor and are headed out to sea."

Crenshaw was furious. "We've been *shanghaied* in the Yucatán!"

"Ollie, don't make a scene," Aunt Alex scolded. "We wanted to come on this trip, remember? We all were looking forward to it, and I'm sure we'll have a lovely cruise."

"But we were lured here on false pretenses," he argued. "You thought you'd come to solve a *crime*."

"A crime will soon be committed," said Mr. Kulcan. "For the next three days I'd advise you to be alert to all dangers."

"What kind of dangers?" asked Cassie.

"Expect the unexpected," he advised. Mr. Kulcan bowed and walked away.

"I don't like this," said Crenshaw uneasily.

"Shame on you, Ollie," said Aunt Alex. "You don't really think Mr. Kulcan *lured* us here, do you?"

"Well, what do *you* think?"

"I think Mr. Kulcan wanted one last chance to change my mind about giving him the necklace," said Aunt Alex. "I'm sure he sent us that invitation as a friendly gesture. You can catch more flies with *honey*, Ollie. Mr. Kulcan hoped his generosity would be rewarded by my giving him the necklace."

"You think so?" asked Cassie.

"Maybe," said Crenshaw. "But maybe he plans to *trick* you out of that necklace."

44

"He can't trick *me*," said Cassie. "As long as that necklace is mine, *no one* gets it!"

Cassie and Barney strolled across the recreation deck after dinner.

"Crenshaw really blew his stack tonight," said Barney.

"I don't blame him," said Cassie. "*I* think there's something strange about this cruise, too. Mr. Kulcan is hiding something, and I wonder what it is."

"Like I told you, it's a mummy's curse," Barney teased. "Mummies always return from the grave to get what they want, and you've got it, Cass. I'll bet those Mayan glyphs we saw were *curses* to protect their stuff, same as those Egyptians had. Maybe you'd better give up that necklace."

"No way."

"Then maybe you should abandon ship. Pull the emergency cord."

"Cords are on trains, you twit. Besides, there's also something *fascinating* about this cruise which makes me want to stay."

"You mean Juan, right? Forget it, Cass, you don't stand a chance with that guy."

"Says who, birdbrain? I'm actually *très, très charmante*, everyone thinks so. I have *finesse, bel air, bon ton. You're* the only creep who doesn't know it!"

"Sure, I'll bet."

"Okay, go ahead," said Cassie. "I'll bet Juan asks me to the dance long before Nena knows you're alive. Nena's too old for you anyway. She'd never waste time with a baby like you."

"I *like* older women," Barney insisted, certain Nena liked him, too. "You've got a deal. Now we've all got bets. It'll be the guys against the girls: me and Crenshaw against you and Aunt Al. What an easy win!"

"You haven't won yet," said Cassie. She suddenly shivered. "It's getting cold up here. I'm going to my cabin."

"Remember what Mr. Kulcan told us," said Barney. "*Anything* can happen on this cruise, so beware."

"*You* remember it, Prescott. Anything can happen to you, too."

"Such as?"

"Such as being thrown overboard—or being frightened to death!"

"Very funny," said Barney.

"I warn you, be on your guard," said Cassie. Then she hurried away.

Chapter Seven

BARNEY HAD NEVER SLEPT ON A SHIP. HE QUICKLY DIS-
covered he couldn't sleep at sea. Although the
Quetzal was a sturdy old vessel, he couldn't get
used to its pitching back and forth. The deck lights
shone through his porthole, so he spent a restless
night.

Just before dawn he fell asleep. Happily he
dreamed of Nena. . . .

. . . They were seated on deck together. "Barney," said Nena (in a lovely Latin accent), "you
are so very handsome."

"I know," he said.

"I think maybe I *love* you."

"You should," he said.

Nena popped grapes into Barney's mouth, then fanned him. "I think you are almost *perfect*."

"You're right," he said.

They held hands as they stared out to sea. . . .

It was a *wonderful* dream!

Unfortunately it was followed by another, not so pleasant. At least Barney thought it was a dream, one of those fuzzy, restless ones somewhere between sleep and wakefulness. . . .

. . . Someone was in the cabin standing in the shadows by the foot of his bunk. It was someone with a grotesque misshapen face, sharp teeth, and bulging eyes. Was it the face of an animal, or was it a skull?

"Who are you?" asked Barney.

The ugly creature groaned and stamped its one foot. Where the other foot should have been there was a black mirror instead. "I am Tezcatlipoca, demon of black magic and devilry."

"How did you lose your foot?" asked Barney.

"It was torn off by the earth monster when the doors of the dark underworld closed upon me." The demon removed the mirror and held it up for Barney to see.

Barney stared into it. The mirror smoked like an evaporating lake of burning water. "I see only darkness," he said.

The demon rattled the mirror. "In my realm

there is only darkness. The sun never shines in my universe. Look closer," he ordered.

Barney stared into the black and smoke. He saw a dead man's bones.

"I thirst for your heart, so you must be sacrificed," said the demon. "My brother is too lenient. You are the chosen one. Prepare to die at the Toxcatl Festival. Only two more days of life are yours."

Barney fidgeted in his bunk. Two more days of life didn't sound too hot! This dream had to end! He rubbed his eyes, then opened them.

The demon was *still there*! He was standing at the foot of his bunk, still rattling his mirror.

Barney suddenly realized his vision wasn't a dream at all!

There was an *intruder* in his room!

"Who's there?" he shouted.

There was no reply.

Barney trembled with fright. "Who are you?" he asked.

"I am the demon with the mirrored foot," a groaning voice replied. "I have come for your blood!"

Barney was petrified. He hid his head under the covers.

Soon, Barney's common sense gained control.

There couldn't be a real *demon* in his cabin. That meant it must be a *trick*. But who would play such a rotten, stinking, scary trick!

Cassie, that's who!

Barney pulled down the blanket. "I know who you are," he shouted.

The figure raised its hand above its head. It was holding a long sharp *dagger*.

"Come off it, Cass," he yelled. "A joke's a joke, but you've gone too far. You can't scare me with this stuff."

Barney jumped up and lunged toward the edge of his bunk. In a flash the figure dropped the dagger, hurried to the cabin door, then ran down the corridor.

By the time Barney reached the door, the intruder was gone.

"You don't fool me for a minute," he shouted down the corridor. "What a rotten thing to do!" Barney kicked the wall. "This is foul play!" he screamed. "It's not fair!"

Mrs. MacIntosh popped her head out of her cabin door. "What's wrong out here?" she demanded.

Suddenly other guests began opening their doors. They all wanted to know the reason for the disturbance.

A nervous woman introduced herself. "I'm Sarah Quigley. Is this part of the mystery? If so, can't it wait until morning?"

Another guest, Jonathon Jaffrey, was angry. "I thought this was a *pleasure* cruise," he grumbled.

Within minutes a crowd had gathered. The guests who hadn't met during dinner were introducing themselves in the corridor. It was a noisy, confusing mess, with ladies in curlers, people throwing on robes, and lots of yawning.

Someone finally sent for the steward.

The steward informed the captain.

No one knew what'd happened.

At last Crenshaw and Aunt Alex joined the crowd. When Aunt Alex noticed Barney was the center of the chaos, she pushed her way through. "I'll get to the bottom of this. What's wrong?"

"Cassie did it," Barney insisted. "She hid in my room, jumped out at me, then ran away. I nearly died of fright!"

"Why would Cassie do that?" asked Aunt Alex.

"Ask her!" Barney shouted.

"She's not here," said Aunt Alex, glancing around.

"Then *find* her," Mrs. MacIntosh insisted, "or we'll never get back to sleep."

"Let's check her cabin," said Crenshaw.

Everyone hurried down the corridor to knock on Cassie's cabin door.

"Do you think we've found our first *clue*?" asked Sarah Quigley. "Maybe that girl is part of the mystery plot."

"Don't be silly," said Aunt Alex. "Cassie is my *niece*, not a clue." She tapped on Cassie's door, then opened it.

Cassie was fast asleep.

"She's *faking*," Barney insisted. "Dump water on her and see! Cassie was in my cabin wearing that Tezzy mask. She must've stolen it from one of the dancers."

"Impossible," said Captain Merado. "All the dancers left the ship before we sailed, and they took their costumes with them."

With so much noise in her cabin, Cassie woke up. Startled, she sat up and grabbed her covers. "What's going on? What're you doing in here?"

"Did you sneak into Barney's cabin?" asked Crenshaw.

"I've been *sleeping*."

"Liar!" Barney shouted. "You were carrying a *dagger*. I saw you."

"You're a mental case," said Cassie. "I've been asleep for ages."

"Then perhaps this *is* our first clue," said Aunt Alex. "We'd better check your cabin, Barney."

52

Now *everyone* was anxious to see Barney's cabin and the possible first clue. They hurried down the corridor to take a look.

Captain Merado switched on the light.

The dagger was lying at the foot of Barney's bed.

"See, I told you," said Barney.

Aunt Alex picked up the dagger. "I think we should check it for fingerprints."

Sarah Quigley grabbed the weapon. "Let *me* see."

"You've smudged the fingerprints," said Aunt Alex. "Now they're ruined."

Sarah Quigley blushed with embarrassment. "I'm sorry. This is my *first* mystery."

All the passengers stared at the dagger. The handle was made of mosaic tiles, and the point was carved from pinkish red stone.

"It looks very old," said Mrs. MacIntosh.

"And very deadly," added Mr. Jaffrey.

"I've never seen anything like it," said Sarah Quigley.

"I have," said Captain Merado. "It's an ancient sacrificial dagger."

"You mean it's used to *kill* people?" asked Barney.

"It was used to cut out their hearts," explained the captain.

Barney gulped. "If Cassie didn't leave it here, then who did?"

"This dagger must be our first clue," said Aunt Alex. "But we still don't know what the mystery is."

"Why was it dumped in *my* cabin?" asked Barney.

"Let's ask Mr. Kulcan," said Crenshaw. "After all, this is *his* little party."

As the passengers hurried down the corridor, Nena and Juan Esperanza appeared. They wanted to know what was happening, too.

"We're looking for Mr. Kulcan," Crenshaw explained. "We've discovered our first clue, but the mystery is still a mystery!"

An hour later the ship had been searched.

Mr. Kulcan couldn't be found on board.

"That's impossible," said Crenshaw. "He's our host. He was here when we sailed, so he couldn't have *disappeared*."

"It's very puzzling," said Captain Merado.

"Then that's our mystery!" said Aunt Alex. "We're supposed to discover where Mr. Kulcan is hiding."

"How?" asked Barney.

"By examining our clues," said Aunt Alex.

"We have only *one* clue," said Crenshaw.

"The dagger," said Barney.

"Where'd it go?" asked Cassie.

"I've placed it on the upper deck for everyone to examine," said Captain Merado. "My written instructions say all clues must be on display."

"Things finally make sense," said Aunt Alex.

"Not to me," said Cassie.

"Mr. Kulcan must be our mystery," explained Aunt Alex. "He gathered us all here in order for us to find him."

"You mean he's playing hide-and-seek with us?" asked Barney.

"That doesn't make sense," said Crenshaw. "The ship has already been searched."

"Good mysteries never make sense at first," said Aunt Alex. She took several deep breaths. "There's nothing better than an early-morning sea breeze to clear the head. Breathe deeply, children. And keep your eyes and ears open. The fun has just begun. I knew this cruise would be exciting. I can hardly wait to see what happens next!"

Barney was starving. It was still too early for breakfast, so he returned to his cabin.

The entire mystery was much too weird for him! Besides, he didn't like being singled out.

Exactly *who* had been in his room anyway? If it wasn't Cassie, then who was it? Mr. Kulcan maybe? But why would Mr. Kulcan dress up like that Tezzy demon? And why'd he pick *him*? After all, *Cassie* had the necklace, why not scare *her* instead?

As Barney sat on the edge of his bunk, he noticed something on the floor. It was something which had gone undetected when everyone had hurried into his cabin.

In the corner by the porthole he saw several footprints.

Barney knelt and examined them more closely.

The prints had been made by one right foot.

Whoever had sneaked into Barney's room had only one leg!

What did *that* mean? he wondered.

Suddenly he had a disturbing thought. Tezcatlipoca, the *real* demon with the mirrored foot, had only one leg!

So what? Tezzy was a myth, an imaginary being—nothing to be afraid of, right?

Barney rubbed his eyes. When he stared down at the floor again, he saw the footprints begin to *disappear*.

Another disturbing thought crossed his mind. Tezcatlipoca could make himself *invisible*.

Barney ran into the bathroom. Was he going

nuts or what? He washed his face with cold water, then stared at himself in the mirror. He looked perfectly normal.

"Hunger must be making me delirious," he told himself.

Then he hurried out of his cabin to get himself some breakfast.

Chapter Eight

AFTER BREAKFAST AUNT ALEX SAT ON THE SUN DECK with her knitting.

Cassie sat beside her, sunbathing. "What are you making?" she asked.

"Nothing," Aunt Alex admitted. "I'm *spying,* hoping more clues will pop up."

Cassie giggled. "I'm not really sunbathing either. I'm waiting for Juan. I hope he strolls by and sees me in my new bathing suit."

"Very clever, Cassie; you'd make a good criminal."

"Aunt Alex, why do you like mysteries so much?"

"I love the *adventure.* It's the thrill of the chase and not knowing how things will work out."

"I guess that's why I like *boys*," said Cassie.

Aunt Alex handed her some suntan lotion. "Here, grease your nose before Juan arrives."

Crenshaw returned from his morning stroll around the deck. "Everything seems shipshape on board, but there's no sign of Mr. Kulcan."

"Did you find any new clues, Ollie?"

"I'm not interested in clues, Alex. I'd rather learn more about that dagger. I think I'll check the ship's library."

Charlie Hackett walked by and waved hello. "Morning, ladies, what'd you think of breakfast?"

"Too much corn," Cassie complained. "Corn muffins, corn *everything*."

"Yeah," he agreed, "I've got corn coming out of my ears!" Charlie Hackett laughed at his own joke. "No pun intended." Then he jabbed at his teeth with a toothpick. "Why can't we get a good bologna sandwich on this crate?"

"Our invitations promised *ethnic meals*," said Aunt Alex.

"Don't remind me," he grumbled.

Aunt Alex eyed Mr. Hackett suspiciously. "So far I think it's a wonderful mystery cruise, don't you? We've already found the first clue in our whodunit."

Charlie Hackett scowled. "Hogwash!"

"*Excuse* me?"

"Excuse *me*, little lady, but you don't think we've been invited on board to solve a *mystery*, do you?"

"Of course."

"Well, you're dead wrong. We've been *lured* here—tricked—stranded out at sea. Yes, sir, we've all been outsmarted by that creepy little old man."

"Do you mean Mr. Kulcan?" asked Cassie.

"That's right, he tricked us all." Charlie Hackett moved a deck chair closer, then lowered his voice. "I've been doing some *private* investigating. Yes, sir, I've uncovered some interesting facts. Guess how the guests were picked for this jaunt?"

"How?" asked Cassie.

"Everyone on board this freighter owns a piece of *rare Mexican jewelry*."

"Really?"

"That's right, girlie. And everyone's had a visit from Mr. Kulcan recently."

"Yes, Mr. Kulcan came to see *us*," said Cassie. "He asked about my jade necklace."

"Did he expect you to *give* it to him?"

"That's right. He said it'd been stolen a long time ago."

Charlie Hackett slapped his thigh. "What'd I tell you? That old guy is a *con artist*. He told *everyone* that cock-and-bull story. That's what he told my missus, too. He wanted my Gladys to give over her turquoise bracelet to him. Know what she said? 'You're nuts,' that's what. Yes, sir, she sent him on his way."

"We thought he was a little crazy, too," Cassie admitted.

"Crazy like a fox," said Charlie Hackett. "It takes a clever guy to hatch a scheme like this."

"Like what?" asked Aunt Alex.

"Luring us on this crate, then disappearing. Kulcan can't fool me."

"He can't?"

"No, sir, little lady. We haven't been invited onto this crate to snoop for clues and weed out red herrings."

"We haven't?"

"No. We're *victims*."

"We are?"

"Yes, sir. I'll bet you brought that necklace with you, right? Sure, *everyone* brought their jewelry, just like the invitation said. Before we dock, it'll be *stolen*. Old Kulcan is hiding out, waiting for his chance to rip us off!"

"We'd better tell the captain," said Cassie nervously.

"That won't do no good, girlie," said Charlie Hackett, frowning. "I'll bet they're in cahoots.

We're *trapped* on this tug, and there's no way out. Don't say I didn't warn you." He got up and walked away.

Cassie stared after him. "What'll we do, Aunt Alex? Should I return to my cabin to make sure my necklace is safe?"

"Relax, Cassie. You don't believe what Mr. Hackett told us, do you?"

"Sure, don't you?"

"Of course not. I think he made it all up just to throw us off the scent."

"Why would he do that?"

Aunt Alex grinned knowingly. "Look sharp, Cassie. This is a *mystery* cruise, remember? Red herrings will pop up all over. *Actors* are mingling with the guests. Nothing is what it seems to be!"

"You think Mr. Hackett is a red herring?"

"A real ringer. I don't believe he has a wife, Gladys. We haven't seen her, have we? Yes, I'd say Charlie Hackett is a *major* red herring!"

"Really? I'm not sure. What if my necklace isn't safe on board? Maybe I'll run down to the cabin and check."

"Suit yourself," said Aunt Alex, "but I think a charming gentleman is headed your way."

Cassie peered over her sunglasses. Juan Esperanza was strolling across the deck. He looked *très, très* dreamy in white tennis shorts and a polo shirt. "What should I do? If I leave now, I may miss my big chance to flirt—I mean, to meet him."

"*Never* miss a chance to meet a handsome young man, dear," said Aunt Alex.

Juan smiled as he approached.

Cassie smiled back, then slid down onto her lounge. "You're right, I think I'll stay!"

Chapter Nine

THE EARLY-MORNING DISCOVERY OF CLUE NUMBER One had brought all the passengers on deck.

Sarah Quigley leaned overboard, carefully examining the ship's hull. "You never know what you'll find down there," she explained.

Jonathon Jaffrey surveyed the horizon with his binoculars. "I wonder where old Mr. Kulcan disappeared to."

Mrs. MacIntosh was complaining, as usual. "My cabin is on the shady side. Disgraceful!"

Captain Merado descended from the wheelhouse bridge. "I've instructed my engineer to move slowly, about ten knots. Are you all having a pleasant journey?"

"I'm not," said Barney. "I'm still *hungry.*"

Barney longed for some bacon or an egg—anything but *corn.* He walked along B deck, gazing over the Caribbean Sea, listening to his stomach rumble. It sounded louder than the water!

At the end of the promenade deck Barney saw the pool surrounded by deck chairs. *Nena* was seated there. Barney's heart pounded. The sun glistened against her shining black hair. She looked like a genuine Mayan princess for sure!

"Hello, come sit with me," said Nena, waving to him.

"Who, *me?*" he asked stupidly.

Nena laughed and nodded. Barney thought her laugh sounded just like rippling water. His knees turned to mush. Awkwardly he scooted up onto a deck chair.

"The captain told me your name," said Nena. "Hello, Barney."

Barney sighed. (Nena had said his name just the way he'd dreamed it!) His cheeks flushed. What did guys *say* to girls—especially *royal* ones? He stared at the shells, beads, and feathers in Nena's long black hair. "You're very *beautiful.*"

Nena plucked a green feather from her braid and handed it to him. "This comes from the quetzal bird."

"Hey, that's the name of this ship, too. What a coincidence."

"No, nothing happens by chance, Barney. All things are planned long ago. All cycles must be completed."

"Oh yeah?" he asked vaguely. "Hey, are you really a *princess*? Miguel said your family were kings and stuff."

"Yes, my father was a lord. This means he had the great privilege of having his head mummified."

Barney shuddered. "Your people have some weird customs, don't they?"

"Tell me something, Barney. Do you have any scars?"

"Any *what*?"

"Do you have any scars on your body?" asked Nena.

Barney didn't know much about girls, but it seemed a weird question. "Nope, I have no scars. Do you?"

"Are you sure?" asked Nena in great earnest.

"Sure I'm sure. Like my mom always says, I'm practically *perfect*."

Nena was pleased. "And I see you have no blemishes. That's good, Barney. Your eyes are bright and clear, too. You have no scars, no wrinkles, no bulges. I am very happy."

Barney scratched his head. (Girls were even weirder than he'd thought!) "I'm glad you're happy, but why do you ask so many questions about *scars*?"

"I have to make sure you're *perfect*," she explained. "Now I have a present for you."

"For *me*?"

Nena opened the satchel beside her deck chair. She handed Barney a hand-carved wooden flute. "It's very old. I'll teach you to play it."

Barney took the flute and blew through it.

"Not like that," said Nena. She showed him where to place his fingers. "It's very simple, see?"

Barney tried again. A sweet sound emerged. "Hey, you're right, it's real easy." He began to play.

Nena nodded approvingly. "You're very clever, Barney. Yes, you are perfect in every respect."

"Hey, thanks a lot, Nena!"

"I have many more gifts for you." Nena removed a wicker hamper from her satchel.

Barney's stomach rumbled loudly. "Is that *real* food? It's not more corn, is it?"

Nena opened the hamper. Inside were oranges, grapes, luscious melons, and other tropical fruits.

Barney's mouth watered. "I *love* fruit!"

"And I love to make you happy," said Nena, popping a grape into his mouth. "That is my mission."

Barney couldn't believe it. Was he *dreaming* again or what? Everything was happening as he'd imagined. How could he be so lucky? No, it wasn't luck. He was *irresistible*—practically perfect.

As Barney gobbled the grapes, Nena suddenly grew upset. "I've forgotten something. I must go get it."

"Can't you stay?"

"I'll return, I promise." Nena kissed his cheek, then hurried away.

Barney touched his cheek. It burned hot. He stared out to sea in a daze.

Then he noticed Cassie stroll by, arm in arm with Juan. They looked as if they were getting chummy. Who cared? Barney had almost won the bet already!

As Juan stopped to speak with Miguel, Cassie hurried over. "Prepare to lose that bet, creepo," she said smugly. "Juan and I will be an item any minute! It won't be long before he asks me to the dance."

"Too late, you've already lost," said Barney. "Nena is *nuts* about me. She's eating out of my hand, or vice versa. Look, she gave me *presents*." Barney looked for the food and flute, but they were *gone*. "Maybe she took them with her, but she's coming right back."

"You're talking nutsy," said Cassie.

"If you don't believe me, *double* the bet."

"You can't double *nothing*, stupid; we didn't bet anything."

"Let's bet now."

"Name it, wimp!" said Cassie confidently.

Barney thought a moment. What would Cassie *hate* to give him? "I'm sick of you calling me a wimp. Everywhere we go you call me that, so *stop it*."

"You *are* a wimp, so what else should I call you?"

"Call me 'perfectly wonderful Barney.' Call me that for a *whole week*."

"Get real, Prescott; that'd make me *choke*!"

"Is it a bet or not? What's wrong? Afraid you'll *lose*? Maybe Juan doesn't like you after all."

Juan *did* like her; Cassie was *sure* of it. It wouldn't hurt her to take Barney's bumbling bet. "It's a deal, dumbo."

"Good, that's settled."

"Hold it," she said. "What if *you* lose?"

"Then I'll call *you* 'perfect' all week, okay?"

"It's a *stupid* bet, but okay."

Juan returned. "The steward thinks someone found another clue on A deck. Shall we go see, Cassie?"

"Absolutely, Juan, I'm *mad* for mysteries!"

"Liar," Barney said.

Cassie took Juan's arm. "Pay no attention to my wimpy cousin. He's *très, très loco. Quel dommage*, a tragic case!" Cassie sneered, then strolled away.

Barney could see Nena hurrying back across the deck.

"I'm glad you waited," she said. "I forgot my most important gift."

"Hey, you don't have to give me more stuff."

"Yes, all things must be as they must be."

"You talk real strange, Nena."

Nena removed a wooden rack from her satchel and placed it in Barney's lap. "You must keep this," she told him.

"Why, what is it?"

"It is a tzompantli. In two days we will put your red cactus fruit inside."

"We will?"

"Yes. Now promise you'll play your flute tonight." Nena returned the flute to Barney. "In two days you must play it well. It's very important."

"Why? What's so important about two days from now?"

"That is when you end your journey," she told him.

"You mean, this cruise? Hey, there's a big dance our last night. Are you going with your brother?"

"I don't like my brother," said Nena. "We are enemies."

"Really? Sounds like me and Cassie. She's hoping Juan will ask her to the dance. Maybe you and me could go together, too, okay?"

"You may not recognize me at the dance, Barney. I may look very different."

"You mean, you'll have a costume? I think costumes are sissy."

Nena popped more grapes into his mouth. "Sometimes disguises are necessary."

Barney munched happily. "These are great. Got any more?"

"No. Would you like some plums?"

"Sure, Nena, dump them on here."

As Barney held out the wooden rack, Nena grew angry. "No, the tzompantli must be saved for your red cactus fruit!"

Barney began to think foreign girls were *lots* weirder than those back home! "I've never heard of red cactus fruit," he said. "What is it?"

"In two days you will find out," said Nena.

"I don't want the cruise to end so fast," Barney confessed, "not since I met *you*." Barney noticed Nena's eyes begin to cross. Was she tired? Barney's cat, Gertie, had eyes that crossed whenever she was tired. "Did you get enough sleep last night? I didn't. I hope no more clues pop up in my cabin tonight. I need some rest."

"You'll sleep soundly," said Nena. She took a Thermos from the satchel and poured something into a glass.

Barney watched her. "That's a real Mary Poppins bag you've got there!"

Nena handed him the drink. Barney tasted it. It was thick, green, and strong. "Nice. What is it?"

71

"This is a drink given to the god Quetzalcoatl," she explained. "The ancient ones made it from maguey cactus."

Barney yawned. "Yeah, it tastes real gooey."

"Would you like to take me to the dance?" asked Nena.

"Sure, that'd be great."

"Rest now, Barney," she said. "All your wishes will be granted the next two days."

Barney yawned again. "I wish I could sleep."

Nena stroked his forehead. "You will sleep for hours."

Barney's eyelid drooped. He felt the ship sway in rhythm with the water. Slowly Nena's face grew blurry. Her black hair, copper-colored skin, and colored feathers seemed to be *changing*. They were crumbling before his eyes, shifting like the sands of time, like the sands of ancient tombs. Suddenly Nena's face was *gone*. She had turned herself into a skeleton! Pieces of jade rested in the hollows where Nena's eyes once were, green jade like the water, green jade tucked inside Nena's skull, a skull which had been unearthed from the ground after hundreds of years.

"Is that *you*, Nena?" Barney whispered. "You look so *ugly*."

"This is my true image."

"Are you *dead*?"

"Yes, I've been dead for hundreds of years."

"Really? What are you doing *here?*"

The skull's mouth moved. "All things must be as they were. All cycles must be complete. Treasures were stolen from my tomb. They have not been returned, so *you* must be sacrificed. The gods command it."

"I don't want to be sacrificed," Barney whined.

"It must be done," the skull insisted. "You will die at the Toxcatl Festival."

Then the skull crumbled into dust before Barney's eyes.

Barney's body felt like lead. He tried standing up, but he couldn't. Half of him didn't believe what he'd seen. "It's just a dream," he told himself. The other half disagreed. "This is no dream; it's *real.*"

Barney couldn't stay awake any longer. He sank into the deck chair and closed his eyes.

Chapter Ten

". . . A RED-HOT PEPPER," SAID CRENSHAW, SHAKING Barney's shoulder.

"What?" asked Barney, waking up.

"That's what your nose looks like," he explained. "Get out of the sun before you burn up."

Barney rubbed his eyes. "I must've dozed off."

"You've been asleep for hours!" Crenshaw told him. "You missed lunch and a lecture. You also missed Alex make a fool of herself. She thought she'd found Mr. Kulcan hiding in the ship's galley, but it was only the cook taking a nap." Crenshaw sighed. "I'm afraid Alex will *never* win this bet. I thought I'd drop a few clues around myself to make things easier for her, but that would probably confuse her. This cruise is confusing enough already! I'll bet everything happening is tied up with ancient Mayan culture. Our first clue is an ancient sacrificial dagger, right? If I were a superstitious man, I'd say those Mayan gods were seeking *revenge*. Anyway, I had a fascinating time in the library. The brain is always hungry for knowledge, Barney, never forget that."

Barney grabbed his aching head. "My brain feels like *busting*."

Crenshaw sat down and opened his book. "The Mayans had a fascinating culture, and their gods were always hungry for human blood. Every month they had a festival. The most interesting was the festival of the fifth month."

Barney groaned. "Go away, Crenshaw, I can't learn anything today. I have an awful headache."

"It was called the Toxcatl Festival," Crenshaw continued.

Suddenly Barney remembered his yucky dream where Nena had turned into a skull. "A skull in a dream said that word to me. Tell me about that Toxy festival. What is it?"

"It's a celebration to honor the god Tezcatlipoca."

"That creepy guy again?"

"He was a popular god," said Crenshaw. "Each year the most worthy male of the village was selected. He had to be perfect: no scars or blemishes, with good manners. Once he was picked, a young maiden would teach him to play the flute."

"That sounds awfully familiar," said Barney. Was that why Nena had given him a flute? Was that why she'd insisted he learn to play it so quickly? Maybe that Toxy ceremony was being celebrated on this ship. Sure, Nena had chosen *him* to be Mr. Perfect. "Tell me more," said Barney.

"Until the day of the festival all the young man's wishes are granted. Banquets and dances are held in his honor. He's treated like a god."

Suddenly all of Nena's weird behavior made perfect sense to Barney. He knew why she'd invited him to the dance. Barney would be the *guest of honor*. "I get it; it's like being prom queen, only you're a guy, right? What happens after the festival? Does this guy get a prize or what?"

"That's the most interesting part," said Crenshaw. "After the festival the young man is placed in a canoe and taken to a temple where the priests await him. There he must break his flute before he enters."

"Then what?" asked Barney eagerly. "What's he get, a trophy? Go on, what happens next?"

"The priests prepare to take his red cactus fruit."

"Nena told me about that. What is it?"

"The human heart," said Crenshaw.

"The human what?"

76

"Mayans called the heart red cactus fruit," said Crenshaw. "It's time for the young man to be offered to Tezcatlipoca. The knife is plunged into his breast, and his heart is ripped out. It's placed in a wooden rack and offered up to the sun."

Barney felt dizzy. "Hold it. You mean, Mr. Perfect gets *sacrificed*?"

"Yes, the Toxcatl Festival is a sacrificial ceremony, Barney."

Barney felt an awful ringing in his ears. "My awful nightmare was *true*!" he gasped. "The skull I saw didn't lie. I'm going to get my heart ripped out! My days are numbered. I've got only two days left." He began moaning uncontrollably.

"You sound intoxicated," said Crenshaw, noticing the cup on the table. "Where'd you get this drink?"

"Nena gave it to me. She called it gooey something."

Crenshaw sniffed it. "I'd call it tequila. No wonder you passed out!"

"You mean I'm *drunk*?" asked Barney. "That's great! If I'm drunk, I probably imagined everything, right? I'm not going to die after all, am I? The skull lied, didn't it? I mean, there wasn't any skull, was there? No one wants my heart, do they?"

Crenshaw sniffed Barney's breath. "You're *sloshed*! What possessed Nena to get you drunk?"

77

"Who cares? As long as I keep my cactus, everything is okay."

"If Nena is playing pranks, the captain should be notified," said Crenshaw. He was about to summon him when Captain Merado hurried toward them.

"Clue Number Two has just been found," he told them. "It's on display on C deck."

"We'd better take a look," said Crenshaw.

Barney hurried after him. It had been real sneaky of Nena to slip him that drink. But Barney forgave her. *Anything* was better than being sacrificed!

Aunt Alex was in the center of the crowd on C deck. "I found it lying on the steps beside the pool," she explained.

"What is it?" asked Jonathon Jaffrey.

"It's awfully ugly," said Mrs. MacIntosh.

"Are you sure it's a clue?" asked Sarah Quigley.

Crenshaw pushed through the crowd to see the object. It was a wooden rack. "That's a tzompantli," he said.

"How fascinating," said Sarah Quigley.

"A tzompantli is a sacrificial skull rack used at the Toxcatl Festival," he explained.

"How strange," said Sarah Quigley. "Now we have a sacrificial knife and a sacrificial rack. What does it mean?"

"I think it means someone is planning a *murder*," said Mr. Jaffrey.

As Barney pushed forward to see the new clue, his knees turned to rubber bands. The ugly thing looked awfully familiar. It was the gift Nena had given him earlier for his "red cactus fruit." So it *was* true. In two days his heart would be resting in that awful zom-thingy. "It wasn't a dream," he groaned. "I didn't imagine it!"

Barney's knees suddenly caved in. He keeled over onto the deck and passed out.

Chapter Eleven

WHEN BARNEY OPENED HIS EYES, HE WAS IN HIS CABIN, in bed. Cassie was seated beside him, impatiently waiting to shove soup in his mouth.

"What kind?" he asked.

"Corn chowder."

"Forget it."

Cassie dumped the spoon into the bowl. "Suit yourself. I didn't volunteer for this. I was drafted. I'm missing a perfectly charming game of shuffle-board with Juan."

Barney clutched his chest. "That's nothing to what I'll soon be missing."

"How come you fainted? Too much sun?"

Barney grabbed Cassie's arm. "I've solved the

mystery, Cass. In two days, there's going to be horrible murder. Someone is getting their heart cut out, and *I* know who the victim is!"

"You think you're right about *everything*, don't you?" Cassie jumped up and began shouting in a horrible singsong, "PerfectlywonderfulBarney. PerfectlywonderfulBarney."

"Don't say that!" he pleaded. "It's an awful curse being perfect, a curse that'll *kill* me!"

"Nena told me you two are going to the dance together," said Cassie. "Juan hasn't asked me yet, so you've won the bet. A deal's a deal, Perfectly-wonderfulBarney. You've *won*, Perfectlywonder-fulBarney."

It sounded like a *death chant*. "I don't want to win," he groaned. "I've changed my mind. I'd rather be a wimp. Say I'm a wimp, Cass, *please*."

"*No*! I won't go back on a bet. I'll call you PerfectlywonderfulBarney for seven whole days!"

"Don't bother, I'll be *dead* in two."

"What's wrong with you? Aren't you thrilled you won? Don't you want to go to the dance with Nena?"

"I never want to see Nena again. She's not what she seems, Cass."

"Nothing is on this cruise. What happened? Is she a red herring? Did you discover she's an actress in disguise?"

"She's in disguise, all right. She's *dead*. Nena is a skeleton, Cass. She died hundreds of years ago!"

Cassie sneered. "You don't say."

"It's *true*," Barney insisted. "Nena is the princess who owned the stolen jade necklace. If she doesn't get her jewelry back, I've got to be *sacrificed*."

"Really, how interesting."

"No kidding, Cass. I'll be stuck in a canoe and dragged to a temple. Then my heart will get ripped out and put in a zom-thingy. I've been picked because I'm perfect. Only perfect guys get sacrificed. Don't you think that *stinks*?"

"You'd better sleep it off," said Cassie. "Crenshaw told me Nena got you *drunk*."

"Listen, Cass, if Nena is a bag of bones, so is her brother. Juan must be hundreds of years old, too!"

"That's okay. I like older men."

"Aren't you going to *help* me?" Barney pleaded.

"No, I'm going to let you sleep."

Cassie smiled to herself, then left Barney's cabin.

Chapter Twelve

AUNT ALEX BUMPED INTO CASSIE IN THE CORRIDOR. "This ship is a hotbed of intrigue," she said excitedly. "I'm on my way to spy on Charlie Hackett!"

As Cassie passed stateroom 7, she heard Sarah Quigley humming to herself.

Cassie continued down the corridor. She heard Mrs. MacIntosh complain to Miguel: "And no freshwater in my carafe, it's disgraceful!"

Cassie passed Nena's stateroom. She could hear Nena shout, "I grow impatient!" Cassie stopped to listen.

Juan's voice answered back. "In two days we shall have the red cactus fruit."

"What if something goes wrong?" asked Nena.

"Then we shall take the girl instead," said Juan. "Someone must be sacrificed. Tezcatlipoca demands it. I've made the necessary arrangements."

What girl? Cassie wondered. What sacrifice? What a strange conversation! Nena and Juan were talking just as crazy as Barney! Cassie was so curious she pressed her ear against the door.

The voices had stopped.

Cassie peered through the keyhole.

She saw no one inside!

Cassie tapped on the cabin door. No one answered. She opened it.

It was *empty*.

Was she *imagining* things? she wondered. Maybe Barney's crazy talk had given her the creeps.

Cassie shook her head, then hurried away.

When Cassie returned to her cabin, a large basket awaited her outside the door. It had a note attached:

X anthos yellow, like your hair
I dolized for
L oveliness, an
O racle
N ever forgotten,
E ver growing, there was
N ever one so fair.

Your great admirer,
Juan Esperanza

It was a *love note*!

Cassie was thrilled. She'd never received a love note from a drooly too-good-to-be-true guy like Juan before!

The message was confusing but poetic. At the bottom, Juan had made a drawing of arrows piercing hearts—a tender valentine.

Cassie picked up the basket. What was inside? Long-stemmed roses? She opened it. To her surprise, it was filled with *unshucked corn*. That wasn't romantic! It's the thought that counts, but she would've preferred *roses*.

Crenshaw came down the corridor, still reading his book. "I got a gift from Juan," she told him proudly. "It came with a *love note*. I think he's insane for me."

Crenshaw read the message. "Just as I thought, Mayan culture is entwined in everything on this ship."

"What's culture to do with it?" asked Cassie.

"Look here, the first letter of each line spells out XILONEN."

"So? What's that?"

"According to my book, Xilonen is the goddess of the tender corn plant."

"Maybe that's why Juan sent me corn instead of roses. You suppose it's a Mexican custom?"

"*Sacrifice* was the custom," Crenshaw explained. "Each year a young female was sacrificed to Xilonen."

"A young *female*? Are you sure?"

"Absolutely. It was an honored tradition. See this picture of knives going through hearts? That's the symbol of the goddess Xilonen."

"I thought those were Cupid's arrows," said Cassie.

"Oh, no," said Crenshaw. "It means a bloody sacrifice."

The basket slipped from Cassie's arms. As the corn fell to the ground, something else dropped out. It landed at her feet with a thud. "What's that?" she asked.

Crenshaw picked it up. "It's another tzompantli. These sacrificial racks are popping up everywhere. Yes, our mystery must involve a bloody sacrifice!"

"*Sacrifice?*" Cassie turned pale. That was the word both Juan and Barney had used. She started running down the corridor. "If someone is getting sacrificed, it's not going to be *me*!"

As Cassie hurried away, she felt angry and confused. What was happening? Was everything part of the mystery?

Cassie didn't like being tricked or made a fool

of. Was Juan being romantic or playing a sick prank? She was determined to find out!

Cassie tapped on Juan's stateroom door. No answer. Inside she could hear loud flute music playing. She knocked again. No reply. She pushed open the door.

Dusk had fallen, and the cabin had grown dark. Cassie saw a figure seated in a swivel chair beside the desk. "Is that you, Juan?" she called out.

No answer.

The flute music grew louder. It seemed to come from everywhere yet nowhere.

Cassie entered the cabin. She approached the chair. "Juan, I have to talk to you." She swirled the chair around.

Cassie screamed as she stared down at the figure in the seat.

It was a *mummy*.

Rotting, ripped wrappings clung loosely to its bleached bones. It sat propped in the chair, as if *waiting* for someone.

Suddenly a voice emerged from inside the mummy. *Juan's* voice. "I see you have discovered my identity."

"Is it *true*? Are you really hundreds of years old?" Cassie whispered.

"All that has been told you is true," the mummy replied. "Soon there will be only one day left before the sacrifice. One day of life before the cycle is complete."

Cassie screamed again, then ran from the room.

Halfway down the hall Charlie Hackett grabbed her. "What's wrong, girlie?"

Cassie was barely able to speak. "It's horrid . . . it's awful . . . it's *frightening*."

Aunt Alex hurried over. "It must be a *clue*. Where is it?"

Breathless, Cassie pointed toward Juan's cabin.

Both Charlie Hackett and Aunt Alex banged on Juan's stateroom door. "Open up in there," Mr. Hackett ordered.

Juan Esperanza appeared at the door. He looked perfectly *normal*. "What's wrong?" he asked.

"There's been a complaint," said Charlie Hackett.

"Oh?" Juan asked with a smile. "What's wrong? Am I playing my music too loudly?"

Cassie stared at Juan. "You're not a *mummy* any longer," she gasped. "How'd you do that? How'd you change back?"

"Cassie, you're not making any sense," said Aunt Alex. "Is something wrong?"

Cassie suddenly felt dizzy. "I don't feel too good," she whispered. "I think I'm going to be sick!"

Chapter Thirteen

WHEN CASSIE OPENED HER EYES, SHE WAS IN HER CABIN, in bed. Barney was seated beside her, waiting to shove soup in her mouth.

"What kind is it?" she asked.

"Corn chowder."

"Skip it," she groaned.

"You almost fainted," said Barney. "Aunt Alex thinks you had too much sun."

"Did Aunt Alex find anything *strange* in Juan's cabin?" asked Cassie.

"Nope, no clues."

Cassie's heart sank. It was *true* then. Juan *could* turn himself into a mummy, then change back into a dreamy guy. What a bitter disappointment!

She grabbed Barney's shoulders. "Listen, I *believe* your wacky story about demon gods and sacrifices. I also believe cousins should stick together. That's why I've decided to help you."

"Why are you volunteering?" asked Barney suspiciously.

"Because I'm a kindhearted soul, you boob!"

"Since when?"

"That's gratitude," Cassie shouted. "I'm offering you my help from the goodness of my heart!"

Barney pushed her aside. "Your *heart*? Hey, I get it! What if I'm not the only one to be sacrificed? Did Juan send *you* one of those zom-thingies, too?"

"What if he did? *You're* still their first choice for sacrifice, so don't push me ahead of you!"

"What happened?" asked Barney. "Did Juan turn into a skeleton, too?"

"A mummy," Cassie told him. "I walked into his cabin, and there he was, all rags and tatters. It was horrible. A few minutes later he was back to normal, handsome as ever. What'll we do, Barns?"

"Simple, give back the necklace. That's what started this whole mess, right? If that Tezzy god gets what he wants, he'll leave our hearts alone."

"It's not so simple," Cassie explained. "Charlie Hackett says *everyone* on board has some stolen Mexican jewelry. We'd have to convince *them all* to give it up."

"Then let's do it," said Barney.

"How? What'll we tell them?"

"The *truth*." Barney sighed. "You're right. Who'd believe it?"

"Maybe we can *trick* them out of their jewelry," said Cassie. "It's for their own good."

"And *ours*," Barney added. "How will we do it?"

Deep in thought, Cassie paced the cabin. "We'll wait until the dinner dance, when everyone will be wearing the jewelry. Then we'll figure out a way to *take* it from them."

"Isn't that *stealing*?" asked Barney.

"It's also a matter of life and death," said Cassie solemnly.

"Whose life and whose death?" asked Barney. "After all, Tezzy only needs *one* sacrifice. If we don't succeed, I wonder which one of us will be murdered."

Cassie was wondering the same thing!

Chapter Fourteen

AUNT ALEX JOGGED ALONG THE RECREATION DECK THE
next day. "Where are the children? I haven't seen
them since breakfast."

"They've turned into supersnoops," said Cren-
shaw. "Cassie and Barney are spying everywhere.
They're cornering passengers, inspecting cabins.
What are they looking for?"

Aunt Alex grinned. "*Clues*, of course. Good. At
last they're getting involved in the mystery."

"No, I don't think they're investigating Mr.
Kulcan's disappearance," said Crenshaw. "I think
it's something more sinister."

"I think you're right, Ollie," she agreed. "There's
something *doubly* fishy about this cruise, isn't

there?" Aunt Alex quickened her pace around the deck. "And I'll be the first to figure it out. So long, Ollie, I'm off to do some supersnooping myself!"

Barney threw his notebook onto the bunk. "There's the complete list of the stolen jewelry on board."

Cassie read down the items: Mrs. MacIntosh, pearl pendant; Jonathon Jaffrey, turquoise ring; Sarah Quigley, jade earrings; etc., etc. . . . "This princess had quite a collection. Good work, Barns."

"*Hard* work," he added. "At first the passengers refused to tell me what they'd brought. But I convinced them that telling me was part of the mystery plot."

"I've been working hard, too," said Cassie. "I found the engine room where they keep the generator. All the electrical boxes down there are labeled. We won't have any trouble cutting off the lights to the main lounge. All we need to do is flip a switch."

"Good, but we can't take chances," said Barney. "We'd better practice our game plan."

"What game plan?"

"This maneuver must run smoothly, just like a football game," he explained. "The Costume Dinner Dance kicks off the game, see? Okay, so we play it cool for the first quarter while everyone eats dinner. But once the dancing begins, we move in for the kickoff. First, you inspect the guests to make sure they're all wearing their jewelry, okay?"

"Okay, then what?"

"Then I'll move everyone toward the end zone," Barney explained. "I'll pretend I found a new clue, okay? This'll be your cue to run to the engine room and switch off the juice. Once the lights are out, I'll start ripping off the jewelry. Touchdown and the game's complete!"

"Wait, what if no one'll give up their jewels?" asked Cassie.

"Then I'll try some block tackles. Listen, don't worry, I'll have the element of surprise. You do your part: throw a monkey wrench into the engine room switch box, okay?"

"Where do I get a wrench?" asked Cassie.

"That's just an *expression*, Cass. Are you *sure* you found the right generator? A ship this size might have two. We can't afford mistakes."

"Sure, I know what I'm doing," she insisted. "Don't worry, I'll get a home run."

"Swell," Barney moaned.

Crenshaw and Aunt Alex were having their evening cocktails on the boat deck. Aunt Alex stared over the glistening water toward the orange sun on the horizon. "The mystery will soon be over, Ollie."

"Good," said Crenshaw. "All this running around makes me nervous."

"I think it's exciting," said Aunt Alex. "It's true adventure. Hugo always said everyone should find adventure in life. Building a financial empire was his adventure. Making fortunes was a magical game to Hugo. For me, mysteries are just as magical."

"Do you think you've solved this one?"

"Not yet," she admitted, "but this makes the game more exciting." Aunt Alex sighed wistfully. "This cruise isn't the only thing that's almost over, Ollie. Soon Cassie and Barney will be leaving us. We'll never have another year like this again."

Crenshaw took her hand. "Never say never, old girl."

"You *do* like the children, after all, don't you, Ollie? At least a tiny bit?"

"I never said so," he snapped, pulling his hand away. "Drink up, it's almost time to dress for dinner. Which means it's almost time I won my bet."

"Who says so?"

"You admitted you haven't solved the mystery. Face it, Alex, it's too late now; this cruise is ending."

"You don't know beans about mysteries, do you, Ollie? Final plot twists are *always* saved for the end. See you in the main lounge in an hour. And expect the *unexpected*!"

Barney tapped on Cassie's stateroom door. "Are you ready?"

"All set."

Barney stared at her. "What's that you're wearing?"

"It's my costume, stupid." Cassie swirled around the room, showing off her yards of sequined ruffles. "Do you like it? It's a Mexican peasant dress. Aunt Alex bought it for me in Mérida."

"Costumes are sissy," said Barney. "I'm just wearing a mask."

Cassie removed the jade necklace from her jewelry box and put it on.

"Hey, put that back," said Barney. "Tonight I'm a *jewel thief*, remember?"

"I have to avoid suspicion," she explained. "Everyone else will be wearing their jewels tonight. If I don't I'll be the first suspect when the theft is discovered."

"Yeah, you're right," he agreed. "Okay, let's synchronize our watches."

"Don't be so dramatic," said Cassie. "Come on, let's go."

Barney suddenly hesitated. "What's the rush? Let's sit awhile instead."

"Why? What's your problem?"

"I'm afraid to see Nena," he admitted. "After all, I'm her potential victim. If things go wrong tonight, I lose a major body part!"

"So? I'm *Juan's* victim, right? We can't let that pile of bones and rags win out over *us*, Barns. We're living flesh and blood."

"For the moment at least. But don't say *blood*."

"Don't wimp out on me now," Cassie insisted. "Our plan will work, I'm *sure* of it!"

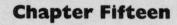

Chapter Fifteen

BARNEY PAUSED OUTSIDE THE MAIN LOUNGE. EERIE flute music filled the corridor. "It sounds like a *funeral.*"

"Keep moving." Cassie pushed him through the door, putting on her mask as they entered.

Inside, the dining room was draped in colorful feathered valances. Two musicians in Indian costumes played their flutes. A heavy scent of incense filled the air. Centerpieces of corn and squash lined the festive buffet tables.

The passengers were in a festive mood as they mingled and sampled the exotic foods.

Barney glanced around. Who was who? He

couldn't recognize anyone in costumes and masks. Barney pointed to a masked man in a bolero jacket, leather trousers, and a straw hat. "Is that Crenshaw?"

"I'm not sure," said Cassie. "What'd I tell you, *everyone's* wearing a costume except you, bozo."

"Who cares what they're wearing? Have they got their *jewelry?*"

"I'll check," said Cassie. Casually she strolled among the guests.

Barney's knees weakened. *Nena* was approaching. No mask or costume could disguise *her*; she looked like a princess, as always. She wore a long white dress belted in gold. Gold chains hung from her neck, and a headband of pearls encircled her forehead. She moved closer. "Have you learned to play your flute? Are you prepared for the end of your journey?"

Nena touched his hand, and Barney grew dizzy. Her beauty hypnotized him. He stared into her eyes. But suddenly Nena's eyes seemed to fade, and he saw two skull holes, instead. Inside the holes a horrible vision unfolded. . . . Time had stopped somewhere long ago. Many men climbed the steps of a Mayan pyramid. Blood ran beneath their feet. At the top of the pyramid each man held a pulsating heart up toward the sun. This completed their bloody ritual. . . . Barney turned away. "I know who you really are," he said. "You're the princess from the Mayan tomb. You're not alive; you're dead. And you're not young; you're old. The Tezzy demon sent you here."

"Tezcatlipoca is no demon," said Nena. "We Mayans knew light cannot exist without darkness. Good and evil will always be at odds. Accept the two forces of nature, Barney; *yield* to them."

Barney clutched his chest. "No way. You'll get your jewelry back tonight, I promise. You're not putting my heart in that zom-thingy! I won't go near a canoe, and I won't be sacrificed, understand? It's no deal, get it?"

"All things will be as they must." Nena left to mingle with the other guests.

Barney grabbed Cassie. "That was a close call. Nena's beauty is only skin-deep, Cass. The trouble is, she has no skin! Don't ever look into her eyes; it's yucky inside there!"

A gong sounded loudly on the upper deck. All the guests turned toward the door as the steward entered. "Attention, passengers, your time is up," he announced. "All the clues have been found; the mystery has ended. Please gather on the main deck after the dance to see if anyone has won the prize."

The masked man in the bolero jacket slapped Barney on the back. "The witching hour is at hand!"

"Crenshaw, is that *you*?"

"I'm not sure who *anyone* is tonight," he admitted, "but I must find Alex and collect my bet."

Barney drew Cassie aside. "It's time the lights went out," he whispered. "Sneak down to the engine room."

"Hold it, I've got bad news," said Cassie. "None of the guests is wearing their jewelry tonight."

"*What?* That's impossible. How come?"

"Charlie Hackett talked them all out of it."

"Why?"

"He warned them they'd be robbed if they did."

"How'd he know that?" asked Barney. "Cass, did you spill the beans?"

"Of course not. Charlie Hackett thinks *Mr. Kulcan* plans to rob us. He convinced them to leave their jewels locked in their cabins."

Barney felt like fainting again. "If we don't give Nena back her stuff tonight, I'm a dead duck! My goose is cooked! My fish is fried! My time is up, Cass. What'll I do?"

"Stop being a selfish pig. *I've* got a heart, too," she reminded him, "but I plan to *keep* mine!"

"How?"

"If we can't steal back the jewelry, let's steal the murder weapon instead."

"The dagger?"

"That's right," said Cassie. "If the dagger disappears, we can't have our hearts cut out with it, right?"

"Good idea," said Barney. "The dagger is on the upper deck. Let's get it."

Cassie and Barney hurried to the door. But Captain Merado pushed them aside as he rushed into the main lounge. He was out of breath and frantic. "There's a fire on board ship!" he shouted.

"Quit kidding," someone told him.

"No more tricks," said someone else. "The mystery is over."

"I'm *serious*. The lower deck is already filled with smoke."

"Impossible," said Crenshaw. "Turn on the sprinkler system. Where's the tank?"

"The cutoff valve is jammed," said the captain. "It won't work. I'm afraid we'll have to abandon ship."

"Nonsense," one guest argued. "I'll bet this is another trick."

"No," Captain Merado protested. "For your safety, you must leave this ship at once. Follow me toward the lifeboats."

Everyone quickly realized the danger was real. The stewards instantly abandoned their food trays to help assemble the passengers into an orderly line. Before they'd reached the dining room exit, the lights suddenly went out. The entire ship was plunged into darkness.

The smell of smoke soon filled the main lounge. The passengers began to panic. They pushed and shoved and knocked each other down in a frantic effort to escape!

Chapter Sixteen

"CASSIE, WHERE ARE YOU?" BARNEY SHOUTED, GROPING his way past the overturned buffet tables.

Through the darkness the captain shouted, "Some of you use the side exits!"

Barney couldn't find any exit. Tripping over chairs and broken dishes, he fumbled through the darkness.

The smoke was getting thicker. Barney covered his face with his hand. Then he felt someone else's hand take his. "Follow me," the voice insisted. Someone grabbed his wrist and led him through the smoky darkness.

They reached the exit door. They hurried along the ship's corridor, up the stairs, and out onto the freedom of the deck.

Barney thought he'd be grateful for fresh air, but an eerie sight awaited him. Smoke enveloped everything on deck, as if the ship were struggling through an impenetrable fog. The night air flowed thickly hot on his skin. Not a twinge of vibration touched the stillness of the vessel.

Peering through the fog, Barney was barely able to see. Everything seemed like a nightmare. Farther aft Barney could hear the other passengers choking for breath. "Did everyone get out okay?" he shouted. "Cassie, Aunt Alex, where are you?"

A hand grabbed his wrist tightly. "Come this way," the voice commanded.

In the clouded mist of moonlight Barney got a glimpse of the lifeboat which had been dropped over the ship's side.

"Come along," the voice demanded. "Get in quickly."

As the clouds passed overhead, Barney finally saw his companion. He was dressed like a native chieftain, his black hair tied in a gold band. He wore a feathered headdress, gold armor on his chest, gold bracelets on his wrists. Draped across his shoulder were a spear, a shield, and arrows. A jade mask concealed his face.

"Who are you?" asked Barney.

"I am Tezcatlipoca. Get into the canoe."

Barney froze dead in his steps.

"The time has come," the voice insisted. He held up a black mirror, and black smoke poured from inside the glass.

"You're the Tezzy demon come to life!" Barney gasped. This time he knew it wasn't a nightmare or a vision; it was *real*. Barney knew the lifeboat wasn't meant to save him but to destroy him. If he got in, he'd be rowed out to the temple, where someone would rip out his heart! "No, I won't go with you!" he shouted.

Then Barney panicked. In a frantic effort to escape, he ran toward the stairs.

"You can't escape that way," the voice yelled, then hurried after him.

Barney could hear the demon's footsteps coming closer. He quickly grabbed Barney around the waist, tackling him to the ground.

Tezcatlipoca picked him up.

Barney kicked and screamed, but there was no escape.

Barney stared into the demon's inhuman stony face.

Tezcatlipoca dropped him overboard into the lifeboat.

In that moment Barney knew he was *doomed*!

"Barney, where are you?" Cassie shouted. She was with the group that'd escaped through the main exit. She now clung to the end of the human chain they'd made around the upper deck.

The second mate tried to keep everyone calm. "Remove your masks, and get some air," he suggested.

The passengers quickly ripped off their disguises. With their masks removed, Cassie could finally identify everyone. She glanced over the group. Where was Aunt Alex?

Sarah Quigley leaned over the side, seized by a violent coughing fit.

Mrs. MacIntosh patted her back. "What a hideous cruise. I plan to *sue!*"

Miguel passed among the passengers. "Did everyone get out safely?"

"No, I can't find anyone," said Cassie.

"Don't worry, Mr. Crenshaw is aft helping detach the lifeboats," he explained. "Your cousin is already safely off the ship."

"What about Aunt Alex?"

"I'll check," said Miguel. Moments later he returned with disturbing news. "No one has seen Mrs. Ludlington."

"Maybe she's still belowdecks," Cassie shouted. She ran toward the stairs leading back to the main lounge.

"No, don't go back down there!" Miguel called out.

Cassie ignored him. Determined to find Aunt Alex, she pushed her way through the darkness.

Thick, smelly smoke clogged the ship's corridor as Cassie hurried toward the main lounge. Reaching the dining room, she stumbled over broken dishes and overturned furniture, searching frantically. "Aunt Alex, where are you?"

Could Aunt Alex be lying somewhere, unconscious? Was she injured? In the blinding darkness Cassie couldn't be sure. She felt helpless.

As Cassie ran back toward the stairs, she found the door at the end of the stairwell had suddenly jammed! She banged on it until her knuckles were bruised, but it wouldn't budge.

Smoke rose along the darkened stairway. As she leaned over the railing, Cassie noticed a faint beam of light vanish into the blackness below.

"Is someone down there?" she called out.

There was no answer.

Cassie followed the light. She hurried down the stairs toward the next level. Cautiously she groped her way past the cargo hatches. She felt the heat grow more intense. Was she approaching the source of the fire?

Cassie moved toward the lowest level, still following the light. Midway she tripped on something. She bent down to pick it up. She fingered the object. It was the *sacrificial dagger*. Cassie took another step, then stumbled on something else. When she picked it up, she knew at once it was the *sacrificial rack*. What were they doing *here*?

Suddenly a horrible thought struck her. Was this all part of the plot? Had she been tricked, trapped, *lured* into coming down here? By Juan? Was Juan waiting for her at the end of that beam of light? Waiting to cut out her heart?

Cassie tiptoed down the remaining steps.

She slid her back against the wall as she neared the engine room.

All was silent. The diesel engines had stopped. The ship was dead in the water. The exit door was locked. There was no turning back now.

Cassie followed the beam of light toward the door of the engine room.

"You can't escape," a voice called out inside. "It's all over!"

The door swung open. The beam of light filled the darkened corridor.

A hideous mummy in rotting rags stood in the doorway.

Cassie screamed as it approached her.

Chapter Seventeen

"CATCH HIM!" A VOICE CALLED OUT.

Cassie stood frozen, too frightened to move.

Then she realized she still had the rack and dagger in her hands. She threw them both. The dagger missed its mark, flying over the mummy's head. But the wooden rack hit him smack between the eyes. He groaned, then slipped to the ground.

"Good shot!" shouted Aunt Alex. She stood in the doorway, flashlight in hand, looking pleased and triumphant. "Congratulations, Cassie."

Cassie was stunned. "What are *you* doing here? The ship is on fire, Aunt Alex. We've got to get out!"

"Nonsense, there's no fire. That was just a red herring." Aunt Alex approached the mummy. He lay unconscious on the ground. Bending down, she flashed the light in his eyes.

"Don't touch him," Cassie cautioned. "He's a *demon!*"

"He's a *crook.*" Aunt Alex unwrapped the bandages from the mummy's face.

Cassie couldn't bear to look. She screamed, then hid her eyes.

"Don't be frightened," said Aunt Alex. "These mummy wrappings are just a costume. Don't you want to see whodunit, Cassie?"

Cassie peeked out between her fingers. She didn't see dried-up bones and rotting flesh beneath the mummy's wrappings. She didn't see Juan either. It was *Charlie Hackett.* "I thought it was a *monster,*" Cassie explained. "Did I hurt him? Will he be all right?"

"Yes, he's coming around," said Aunt Alex.

"What's going on here?" asked Cassie.

"Simple, I've solved the mystery," said Aunt Alex proudly. "Charlie Hackett was my prime suspect from the beginning, remember? When he began scaring everyone on board, I knew he was the culprit. I knew he must have an ulterior motive, so I started following him."

111

Charlie Hackett opened his eyes. "What hit me?" he asked, rubbing his head.

"I wish *I* had," said Aunt Alex. Restraining him, she sat on his knees to undo his mummy wrappings. "There's still one unsolved element to this mystery," she said, beginning to unwind his bandages. As she did, pieces of jewelry dropped to the ground.

Cassie recognized the jewelry at once. "That's Mrs. MacIntosh's pearl pendant. And that's Mr. Jaffrey's turquoise ring." One by one the Mayan jewelry on Barney's list came dropping out of Charlie Hackett's mummy wrappings.

"Just as I thought," said Aunt Alex. "What a clever place to stash the loot. And what a clever plan. First you set fire to the ship; then you jump in a lifeboat with the rest of us. We'd be so grateful to be alive we'd never think about our missing jewels. We'd assume everything was destroyed in the fire, and you'd walk away with a fortune. And no one would suspect you'd stolen it."

Cassie noticed the smell of smoke growing stronger. "There *is* a fire, Aunt Alex; let's hurry out of here!"

"Relax," said Aunt Alex, "that's only the last of Mr. Hackett's smudge pots. Where there's smoke, there isn't always fire, Cassie. We caught Mr. Hackett before he set the *real* fire. The smudge pots were to scare everyone into thinking there was a fire. While the passengers were escaping, Mr. Hackett was busy ransacking their cabins."

Charlie Hackett struggled to get up. "You're crazy!" he shouted.

"And you're a *crook*," said Aunt Alex, firmly holding him down. "While you were breaking into the cabins, I was breaking into yours. I found incriminating papers in your suitcase. I have proof you're a jewel thief, not a hardware salesman. I'll bet when you heard about this cruise, you knew it'd be a great chance to steal jewelry."

"You're nuts," he protested. "I was invited, same as you."

"Yes, that part is true," said Aunt Alex. "But a clever liar always adds an element of truth to his story. You were invited because you own Mayan artifacts. But they were *stolen* like everything else you own."

"You can't prove that," Charlie Hackett shouted. "Someone planted this stuff on me."

"I have lots more evidence," said Aunt Alex. "We'll find your fingerprints on the sprinkler valves. You jammed them so everyone would abandon ship. And your prints will be on the smudge pots, too. You placed them all around the engine room."

Finally freeing himself, Charlie Hackett pushed

113

Aunt Alex aside. He knocked the flashlight from her hand. "You can't nab me. I'm getting out of here." He shoved Cassie to the ground, then hurried down the darkened corridor.

When he reached the stairs, Charlie Hackett ran smack into Captain Merado.

"What are you people doing down here?" asked the captain. "Abandon ship at once!"

"Hold that man," Aunt Alex shouted. "I figured out whodunit. I want my prize!"

"Don't listen, she's loony," said Charlie Hackett.

"No, she's not," said Cassie. She picked up all the jewelry from the ground. "Mr. Hackett is a *thief*, and here's the evidence. Aunt Alex is right. She solved the mystery."

Chapter Eighteen

"WHAT A WIMP!" SAID CASSIE. SHE WAS FANNING Barney with a magazine as he lay on the deck of the *Quetzal*. He was wet, limp, and groggy. "Wake up, dumbo, the mystery is over."

Barney opened his eyes. "It's over?"

"Yes, you fool, you missed all the good parts. We had to drag you out of the lifeboat like a dead mackerel. You *fainted* again."

"I did?" Barney felt himself all over. Everything was still there: his head; his heart; everything. He glanced around. "Where'd that Tezzy demon go?"

Cassie threw the magazine at him. "I must've been nuts to believe your wacky story about demons. The mystery is solved. Everything has a perfectly logical explanation."

"Really?"

"Sure, Aunt Alex solved it all, just like she said she would."

"Really?"

Cassie stared into Barney's eyes. "Is anyone in there?"

"I *saw* that Tezzy demon," said Barney, still dazed. "He threw me into a lifeboat."

"That must've been one of the passengers," said Cassie.

"Really?"

"Sure, you admitted you couldn't recognize anyone in their disguises."

"But he threw me *overboard*," said Barney.

"Stop complaining. Be grateful someone tried to save your life. It was all a waste of time, though. There wasn't any fire, only smoke."

Sarah Quigley passed by to offer Barney a glass of water. "Oh, dear, perhaps you've had enough water. Poor thing, you look half drowned."

"I *am*," he told her.

"Hasn't it all been exciting? I've enjoyed every moment, even the pretend fire. People *learn* about themselves under adverse conditions, don't you agree? I've learned a lot, haven't you?"

"No, I haven't," said Barney.

"Oh?" asked Sarah Quigley. "Perhaps a frail child like you shouldn't be on this adventure cruise."

Cassie agreed. "That's right, he's a *wimp*."

"I *love* being a wimp," said Barney. "In fact, I never want to be called perfect again!"

Jonathon Jaffrey interrupted his stroll to inquire about Barney. "Feeling better, lad?"

"No," he grumbled.

"I'll bet you're disappointed you didn't win the prize, eh? So am I. But it's been quite an experience anyway, hasn't it?"

Sarah Quigley agreed. "I'm so glad we all decided to return our jewelry to the Mexican government."

"When did you decide that?" asked Cassie.

"We all took a vote," Mr. Jaffrey explained. "Everyone agreed. Maybe we got a different perspective on life when we thought we might die! Possessions don't mean much then, do they? Anyway, I suspect those jewels may be *jinxed*."

"Maybe you're right," said Sarah Quigley. "If I'd known my bracelet was stolen from a tomb, I'd never have bought it!"

Mrs. MacIntosh hurried over. "There you are, Jonny dear. I've been looking for you. Let's have a drinkie-poo together, hmm?"

Mrs. MacIntosh took his arm. Jonathon Jaffrey blushed as they walked away together.

117

"What got into *her*?" asked Cassie.

Sarah Quigley giggled. "A romance has bloomed on board."

"When did that happen?" asked Barney.

"While we were in the lifeboat," she explained. "Isn't it wonderful? I've read about shipboard romances, but I've never witnessed one. Excuse me, I must write all this down in my diary."

"I guess this trip has done *her* lots of good, too," said Cassie. She fingered her jade necklace. "And I suppose it's time I took this off."

"Are you quite prepared to give it up?" asked a familiar voice from behind her.

Cassie turned around. "Mr. Kulcan! Where have you been all this time?"

"Here and there. Never far away."

"We never saw you," said Barney.

Mr. Kulcan smiled mysteriously. "Perhaps you did without knowing it. You were warned to expect the unexpected."

Cassie removed the necklace and handed it to him. "I don't want this anymore. Put it with the rest of the jewels."

"Are you certain?" he asked.

"When I thought Aunt Alex was hurt, I realized how unimportant some things are."

"Then you've learned a valuable lesson," said

Mr. Kulcan. "I'll see this is returned to its rightful owner."

"How?" asked Barney. "That princess is *dead*. Which reminds me, what happened to Nena?"

"And how did you know Mr. Hackett planned to steal, the jewels?" asked Cassie.

"And where is Juan?" asked Barney.

"And who planted that phony mummy in Juan's room?" asked Cassie.

"And who dressed up like the Tezzy demon?" asked Barney.

"You have so many questions," said Mr. Kulcan. "Unfortunately not all of life's questions have answers. Some things always remain a mystery."

"What's that mean?" asked Barney.

"It means it doesn't matter," said Mr. Kulcan. "All that matters is your adventure ended happily."

"Hey, it's just like in the story," said Barney. "Those gods Quetzy and Tezzy kept fighting to see which one would win. This time the good guys won, right?"

Mr. Kulcan smiled. "Yes, Barney, the good guys won—*this time.*"

"And I've won the prize!" shouted Aunt Alex. She ran along the deck, holding a large brass trophy. "Don't you love it? Isn't it the biggest, gaudiest thing you've ever seen? I've going to make Crenshaw keep it polished. That'll be his

119

punishment for losing the bet." She placed the trophy on a table to admire it. "Look, there's a smudge on it already. Hurry up, Ollie, bring your dustcloth!"

Crenshaw slogged along the deck. He stopped beside the trophy and grudgingly polished the smudge away. "This is a ridiculous job for the world's smartest man!" he grumbled.

"If you're so smart, you should've known I'd *win*," Aunt Alex gloated.

"I guess I forgot how determined you can be, Alex."

"I've never seen such a big trophy," said Barney.

"It's a sizable award for a sizable deduction," said Mr. Kulcan.

"It makes up for all the prizes I've never won before," said Aunt Alex, smiling. "You don't really mind polishing it, do you, Ollie?"

"No, Alex, I never go back on a bet. I'm pleased to polish this—this thing."

"Hasn't this cruise been marvelous?" she asked excitedly. "I've learned so much. You know, I'd almost forgotten that *life* is the ultimate adventure."

"I'd forgotten something, too," said Crenshaw. "But I finally remember why your name sounded so familiar, Mr. Kulcan. Kulkulcán is another name for the god Quetzalcoatl."

"Is it?" asked Mr. Kulcan.

"You *know* it is," said Crenshaw. "I'm beginning to wonder if Alex solved the *real* mystery on this cruise. You're quite a mystery yourself."

Aunt Alex poked Crenshaw. "You said you wouldn't go back on our bet, Ollie."

"I'm only inquiring," said Crenshaw. "Don't you think it's odd Mr. Kulcan got his way? Suddenly everyone on board agreed to give back the jewels."

"So what?" asked Aunt Alex.

"So maybe we *were* lured here after all!" said Crenshaw.

"You think so?" asked Barney.

"It's possible," said Crenshaw. "Are you really what you seem, Mr. Kulcan?"

"Is anyone?" he asked. "Charlie Hackett wasn't what he seemed."

"What will happen to Mr. Hackett?" asked Cassie.

"Captain Merado will hand him over to the authorities when we land," said Mr. Kulcan. "It's an ancient Mayan belief that everyone must undergo many trials before gaining knowledge. I hope Mr. Hackett has learned the error of his ways."

"You never told us what happened to Nena and Juan," said Barney.

"They were called away. Captain Merado supplied a boat to take them to the mainland."

"Why did they leave?" asked Cassie.

Mr. Kulcan stared solemnly out to sea. "Nena and Juan have a long voyage before they reach their journey's end. I'll soon be sailing away, too."

"Where are you going?" asked Barney.

"To Mictlan."

"I think I've heard of that place," said Crenshaw. "Where is it?"

"It's very far away. But I'll return—someday." Mr. Kulcan bowed politely. "Excuse me, I must prepare for my departure."

Aunt Alex watched Mr. Kulcan go belowdecks. "I *hate* the idea that everything is ending, Ollie," she said, sighing. "The cruise is over. The mystery is over. And our year of fun and adventure is over, too." She glanced at her trophy. "This prize doesn't seem so important anymore. I'm losing the *real* prize, Ollie. Things will never be the same without Cassie and Barney."

Crenshaw patted her shoulder. "Never say never, old girl." Then he glanced after Mr. Kulcan. "I've just remembered where Mictlan is. It's in the *underworld*."

"You mean Mr. Kulcan is a *crook* after all?" asked Barney.

"I mean the *mythical* underworld," said Crenshaw.

"Mictlan doesn't really exist except in legend. It's said to be the place where Quetzalcoatl lives."

"If it's not real, how can Mr. Kulcan go there?" asked Cassie.

"I don't know. *Nothing* about Mr. Kulcan makes sense. It's a mystery, isn't it?"

"Aunt Alex can solve it," said Barney. "She's a *supersleuth* now—with an award to prove it!"

"You bet," said Aunt Alex. "But no award could be as exciting as having the two of you children live with me."

"Or as puzzling, or frustrating, or confusing," added Crenshaw.

"Does that mean you like us better than your mystery novels?" asked Barney.

"I like you two better than *anything!*" said Aunt Alex.

Crenshaw shrugged. "That's the biggest mystery of all!"

Aunt Alex smiled. "Maybe our year together is almost over, but who knows where the winds might take us next?"

"Does that mean we'll still keep going on trips with you?" asked Barney.

"Don't be so nosy," said Cassie. "It's rude to ask so many questions."

"But I want to *know*," said Barney.

123

Cassie *didn't* want to know. Knowing would spoil all the romance—and the mystery.

Which way *would* the winds take them next? Cassie wondered. Would Barney go back home? Would she return to boarding school?

Cassie stared out over the horizon dreamily. She clung to the hope that their days of fun and adventure with Aunt Alex were only just *beginning*!